One Mad Night

JULIA
LONDON

sourcebooks
casablanca

Published by Sourcebooks Casablanca, an imprint of Sourcebooks, Inc.
P.O. Box 4410, Naperville, Illinois 60567-4410
(630) 961-3900
Fax: (630) 961-2168
www.sourcebooks.com

The Bridesmaid novella was originally published in 2013 in the United
States by Sourcebooks Casablanca, an imprint of Sourcebooks, Inc.

Printed and bound in Canada.
MBP 10 9 8 7 6 5 4 3 2 1

Contents

One Mad Night   1

The Bridesmaid   153

One Mad Night

Chapter 1

New York

SIX HUNDRED DOLLARS WAS A LOT OF MONEY FOR shoes, especially shoes on sale. *Especially* shoes that could not be relied upon to carry a person ten pain-free blocks. Frankly, it was an obscene amount of money for shoes that did nothing but look good.

But oh, how they looked *good*.

They were bronze Manolo Blahnik pointy-toe pumps, with a three-and-a-half-inch heel and a very cool buckle across the top. They were shoes that said, *look at me, I can do this job better than anyone and I am proud of it*. Still, for that kind of money, Chelsea Crawford thought they ought to come with a Segway.

She had elected not to wear them back to the office. Not only was it starting to snow, but she was fairly certain her feet would never survive the short walk in those heels. No, *these* shoes were to wear during her big presentation tomorrow, and were safely tucked away in a silvery paper Bergdorf Goodman bag that dangled daintily from Chelsea's arm as she and her assistant, Farrah, hurried down the street through snow that was beginning to thicken.

They darted into the lobby of the office building of Grabber-Paulson, the advertising agency where Chelsea had worked for six years, and negotiated their way past the coffee stand to the elevators. As they reached the elevator bank, the shiny, silver doors of one car opened, and they hopped inside.

"Hold, please!" Chelsea heard someone yell, and she turned around, prepared to do just that... until she saw who had yelled. It was Ian Rafferty, the bane of her existence. Chelsea waved her fingers at him, then hit the *close* button with such force that Farrah actually glanced up.

"*Hey!*" Ian shouted as the doors began to slide closed, and he suddenly sprinted, almost reaching the doors before they clicked shut.

"That was, like, *rude*," Farrah said to her phone. Because Farrah rarely looked up from her phone. She'd been assimilated.

"It's okay. He'll get another one," Chelsea said as they rocketed up.

"He's cute," Farrah said to her phone. "Why don't you like him?"

Chelsea looked at Farrah. How could she even ask that question? Ian Rafferty was her biggest competition in-house. Ian Rafferty had taken two accounts that by all rights should have been hers. Ian Rafferty thought he was going to get the plum account, the one Chelsea had worked so hard to get. "You remember the Tesla account, right? Campaign for a luxury electric car? The account I've been working on practically around the clock for the last six weeks?" she asked, her voice full of incredulity.

Farrah shrugged. "I guess so. I just think he's cute."

Chelsea rolled her eyes. Grabber-Paulson was one of two finalists for the new Tesla account. Jason Sung, Chelsea's boss, was spearheading the process. If Grabber-Paulson won the account, it was Chelsea's job to manage. Everyone at Grabber-Paulson knew it was her job. She was due, she'd put in her time, she'd worked her way up, slogging through one account after another. She had great ideas, she was a hard worker, and *everyone* knew it was hers...

Except maybe the partners.

The elevator stopped on the eighteenth floor.

A mail guy and his cart ambled on. He smiled at Chelsea and Farrah as they started their ascent again. "How you ladies doing today?" he asked.

"It's snowing," Farrah said to her phone. Chelsea supposed she expected the mail guy to figure out how she was doing from her weather report.

The mail guy was definitely intrigued and tried to chat up Farrah about the weather. "Snowing, huh?" he repeated.

Chelsea fixed her gaze on the digital display above her and ignored the chatter about snow. She was thinking back to the day Jason had called her into his office six weeks ago. He'd been tossing a Nerf basketball into a Nerf hoop above his desk, which then rolled down a little chute back onto his desk, where Jason could pick it up without actually exerting any effort. "Working hard on the Tesla commercial, huh?" he'd said when Chelsea came in. "The partners *love* your work."

"Right." Chelsea had nodded, because that was old news to her. She'd killed it on the Smooth-n-Silky shampoo account. She'd kicked some serious ass on the Westwood All Natural Grocery account. *This* account was hers. This account was the stepping-stone into bigger and better accounts. Big national accounts. It was her move into a corner office and a big pay raise.

"So now, we come in with a great television concept and *bam*, that's it. We're all getting big fat raises," Jason had said cheerfully.

"Yep," Chelsea had responded confidently. She'd shown Jason her ideas for the commercial. He knew exactly how great her concept was, and it was really great. Some of her best work.

Jason caught the Nerf ball and tossed it to Chelsea, who had never been the sporty type and awkwardly batted it away before it hit her in the face.

"Yeah, I'd say this account has your name written all over it, doesn't it? Good work, Chels. Good work."

"Thank you," she'd said, smiling. She didn't mind a little high praise being Nerfed in her direction, but at the time she'd wondered why he'd chosen that moment to deliver it. She could still feel that tiny, slender moment, the distance between knowing that she had this in the bag and then realizing the rug had just been yanked out from under her feet. It wouldn't be the first time.

"There's just one tiny little thing," Jason had said as he'd propped his feet on his cluttered desk.

Chelsea's gut had dropped then, because there was never anything tiny when it came to Jason. "What?"

"The partners think it would be better if we had a little competition in-house. You know, so we get the very *best* ideas."

"Competition for…"

"So we're putting Ian Rafferty on it."

Chelsea's heart had almost dropped to her toes. Ian Rafferty thought he was God's gift to advertising with that Crest smile, longish golden-blond hair, big shoulders, and swoon-worthy blue eyes. But his looks and, admittedly, killer sex appeal aside, Chelsea saw him for what he was—a glitzy showboat. The reason he'd won two of the three accounts that they'd gone head-to-head on over the last several months was because he knew how to charm people, and especially women.

"Jason!" she'd cried. "How can you do that to me?"

"Ian's good, and he was the guy behind the Infiniti commercials at his old job. Did you ever see them? Infiniti sales went up thirty-four percent after those ads started running. That's *awesome*. That's why we lured him away."

Yes, she knew, along with everyone else at Grabber-Paulson, that supposedly Ian was some prize catch in advertising.

"Anyway, he's going to create a spot for the Tesla account too. And then, you know, we'll decide."

Jason lifted his hands above his head and tossed the basketball into the hoop. "Nothing but net."

Chelsea had gaped at him, her head and heart spinning with the betrayal. "What the hell, Jason? I thought this account was essentially mine! *You* said it was my time, my account. *You* said I was the best!"

"You *are* the best! And this *is* your account!" Jason said, catching the ball again. "I mean, it *will* be your account, because I have great confidence in you, Chels. You are the *best*," he'd said again, waving the Nerf to emphasize each word. "Because this guy can't come up with anything nearly as good as what you'll give us, right? Not to worry, Chels. Not to worry." He tossed the ball again. "Damn, I'm good."

Chelsea had wanted to leap across that desk and rip Jason's ears from his head, and if her skirt hadn't been quite so tight, she might have done it. "I can't believe you, Jason," she'd said. "This is exactly what you did to me on the Northeast Banking account. You said it was mine and then gave it to Zimmerman."

"That was different," Jason said cheerfully. "You had a lot going on."

"I could have handled that account and you know it. I've done everything you've ever asked,

Jason. I've spent an entire weekend in this place for the Smooth-n-Silky campaign. I took that damn Mexican restaurant's work home over the holidays. I worked my ass off to help this firm get into the final round for the Tesla account, and now you're telling me you're letting someone else have a shot at *my* account?"

"Chel-*sea*," Jason had said, picking up the basketball again. "You worry too much!" He tossed the Nerf ball again, but this time, Chelsea lunged and intercepted its marshmallow flight through the air, batting it back at Jason with so much force, she thought she felt something pop in her shoulder. It wafted through the air and Jason caught it. "Good arm," he'd said.

Chelsea hadn't said another word, because if she had, she would have said some very unfortunate and unkind things. She'd marched out of his office, ignoring his call for her to come back.

Fortunately, for everyone at work and for her cat, Chelsea had calmed down since then. It really was her account. She really *did* have the best idea. After six years of pouring her life into that firm, she was due.

The elevator came to a halt and the doors slid open. Chelsea slipped out past the mail guy and his cart—and came face-to-face with Ian Rafferty, who was standing at the elevator, one arm braced against the wall. Chelsea came to such an abrupt halt that Farrah collided with her back, almost pushing Chelsea right into Ian.

She swayed back before any physical contact was made and tilted her head up to peer into those blue eyes. He really did have remarkably sexy eyes. They slanted down at the corners, which had the perpetual effect of making him look as if he were trying to seduce whomever he was talking to.

"Oh. Hello, *Ian*," she said.

"Hello, *Chelsea*. I asked you to hold the elevator for me."

"Oh, is *that* what you meant? I'm sorry." She smiled.

Ian's eyes narrowed. "You know," he said on a sigh as his gaze casually wandered the length of her, "I can't figure you out."

Chelsea's pulse did a strange little flutter at his perusal of her and the idea that he was trying to *figure her out*. "We hardly know each other enough for you to even try."

"I know you well enough to know that for reasons that completely elude me, you take a little healthy competition very personally."

"I don't take it personally—"

"Yeah? Then why do you avoid me like I'm

swine flu?" he asked silkily, his gaze settling easily on her mouth.

Chelsea managed not to squirm with the heat that was rising in her. She refused to be sucked in by his sex appeal. She adjusted her stance so that her Bergdorf Goodman bag was in front of her, like a shield. "I don't know, let's see. A, because I'm not one of those girls who melts at your feet, or B, because I have a lot of work to do."

One corner of his lush mouth tipped up in a smile. "Girls melt at my feet?"

Her gaze narrowed. "This may come as something of a shock to your enormous ego, but I don't actually think about you, Ian. I'm too busy."

"*Uh-huh*," Ian said, and he somehow managed to shift closer to her without actually appearing to move. "Listen, Chelsea," he said, his voice going soft. "I'll be honest…I know you really want this account. I know you think you had it wrapped up and Jason's one hundred percent in your court. But we both know Jason is not the most loyal guy in town."

He looked almost sympathetic, and Chelsea could feel herself responding. Because she *did* think she had it wrapped up. Because he was right—Jason was horribly disloyal.

"But the thing is," he said, leaning closer still,

so that she could smell him, could smell his scent, which, in any other place and time, would have been wildly sexy, "you might not have it wrapped up. And it's really not my fault that you've got Chrysler LeBaron Syndrome."

Chelsea had to stop smelling and think a moment. "Chrysler... *What!?*"

"You design car ads for grandmas. But that's no reason to take out your frustrations on me. I can't help that my ideas are creatively superior."

Chelsea gasped with great indignation, and still she couldn't seem to suck enough breath in her lungs. "Hey! I don't have any frustrations, Ian! I'm not the one who has to design ads for adolescent boys to try to win the account."

"I guess that means you think the partners are adolescent boys, since they are the ones who will award the account."

"I did *not* say that—"

"I didn't think so." He had the audacity to remove a strand of windblown hair from her cheek. "Here's some food for thought: there are a lot of people, even those over the age of seventy, who appreciate the features of a car that don't necessarily have to do with safety."

He had seen her ad. *Damn it, he had seen her ad!* Chelsea had a pretty good idea how she was going to throttle Jason Sung. She was going to stuff his Nerf basketball down his throat and crown him with that hoop. "You don't know nearly what you think you know," she said angrily.

"And neither do you. But you will tomorrow," he said with a sultry wink. A wink! As if they were having a friendly debate! "In the meantime, try and be nice," he said, and with a brotherly pat to her shoulder, he turned around and strode for the office doors, his trench coat billowing out behind him.

"I *am* nice, you self-absorbed goat!" Chelsea shouted after him, but he'd already gone through the plate glass doors that marked the entrance to the Grabber-Paulson suite. She could see him at reception, chatting up Hadeetha, who sat just below the big brass agency sign.

Chelsea's pulse was racing from fury and from a couple of sultry Ian Rafferty looks. It took a moment before she noticed Farrah, who had actually managed to lift her gaze from her phone. She was staring wide-eyed at Chelsea. "Wow. You don't *sound* very nice."

"Oh my—will you just come on?" she said irritably and stalked off, yanking open the office suite doors, bound for her cubicle to review her pitch for any signs of Chrysler LeBaron Syndrome.

Chapter 2

THE SHOT IS LONG, A TWO-LANE ROAD WENDING ITS WAY through the mountains. In the far distance, a car is approaching. It's red. A male voice-over: "You know what you need. Performance. Sex appeal." The red Tesla speeds into view. Suddenly we're in slow motion—the driver of the car, a good-looking guy in his thirties, expensive shades, open collar. A blond with a great rack in the passenger seat, gazing adoringly at him, her hand on his chest. The car rolls by, and the man looks out his window, winks at the camera. "It's all right here, in one package. Looks. Performance. And it's good for you. It's good for the world. It's good for all of us." The Tesla fishtails away onto a mountain road, and the blond lets something fly out the window. A bra. The picture fades to the Tesla logo: Tesla. Environmentally conscious sex appeal.

There it was, fifteen seconds of advertising

genius. Chelsea was crazy—there was nothing adolescent about it. This was a campaign that would speak to the thirty- and forty-something hotshots looking for a cool car, but who also wanted to be on the cutting edge of alternative fuels and energy.

"Run it again," Ian said to the kid in the back of the media room. The ad started up again, and Ian could feel a big fat smile spreading across his face as he watched it. When it was over, he looked at Zach Zimmerman, another account guy. "It's good, right?"

"It's better than good, it's *great*," Zach said. "I'd buy that car. I'd *do* that car."

"That's what I'm talking about," Ian said and stood up; he tapped his friend on the shoulder with his fist. "You're going to be my wingman when I get the account."

"I'd rather be your wingman at the W Hotel," Zach said. "There are some hot chicks hanging around that lobby, and I could use you to lure them in."

"It's a date. Just let me get past this presentation, and we'll do it." Ian winked at his friend, gestured for the assistant to lock it all up, and went out, heading back into cube nation.

This presentation was more important than he let Zach—or anyone—know. They'd brought him into this firm because he was so good at what he did, and Ian could, with all due modesty, agree that he was one of the best. Grabber-Paulson had approached him several months ago and told him they wanted him to be the guy who took great ideas and kicked them across the Grand Canyon. They wanted him to be a pitch guy, the face of Grabber-Paulson. Brad Paulson and Jason Sung had wined him and dined him, made him some pretty grand promises about fast-tracking to partner, and paid him a hell of a lot of money to leave the Huntson-Jones Agency.

Over cocktails one night, they'd explained to him that he'd be the "it" guy, that there was only one other person in-house that was good, but still not as good as he was. Her name was Chelsea Crawford. "She's great at some things but not others," Brad had said. "And we're not sure she's right for cars. That's where we want to go."

"Yeah," Jason said cheerfully as he popped some nuts into his mouth. "Chelsea's the type who does all the research and knows what the market is. But when it comes to sex appeal, she doesn't deliver." He popped more nuts into his mouth.

Ian had pictured a middle-aged woman in sensible shoes, someone with thick glasses and a desk lamp to study the graphs and charts of market trends. He knew he could work rings around that faceless woman.

"You know what we need, Ian?" Brad had asked, leaning across the table to him. "We really need to step it up. Give consumers that thing they've never seen, that thing that makes them crazy, that thing that makes them think they *have* to have it. And we think you're the guy to deliver that *oomph*."

In the end, Ian had been persuaded to take the job. He'd given no more thought to Chelsea the researcher until he met her, and damn it if the woman didn't knock his socks off. He wasn't expecting a dark-haired, green-eyed tall drink of water. He wasn't expecting her to have enticing curves and a pair of legs that he kept imagining wrapped around his waist. He didn't get why Jason said she didn't deliver on sex appeal, because in his eyes, she was oozing it.

Chelsea had been friendly, but at the same time, she'd given off a vibe of being too busy, too involved with her life to get to know him. That was cool, he understood it. When they first went up against each other to compete for the Zoot Restaurant account, he'd tried to befriend her. Ian didn't know why—he was competitive, sure, but he didn't live or die by winning an account. He'd thought Chelsea was of the same mind when she'd congratulated him after he landed the account.

But things between them changed, he noticed. She'd been a little cooler toward him after that. And then she'd gotten the Canon camera account, and Ian hadn't liked it. He'd believed his idea to be clearly superior and felt like Jason was throwing Chelsea a bone. It didn't help that when he stopped by her very neat and orderly cubicle to congratulate her, she'd said, "*Booyah!* I win!" And she'd laughed as she'd done a goofy little dance around her cubicle.

The gloves came off when they both went after the Allmen Insurance account. Ian had to hand it to Chelsea—her idea of a day in the life of a hapless American family was good—the family's accidents had touched on all the key selling points for Allmen. But Ian's idea was better, sharper, more in tune with today's society. His idea was to show a teenager who had just gotten his license plowing through a storefront when he forgot to pay attention. It was cute and it hit on that thing that everyone worried about—the cost of insuring teen drivers who were never without a phone.

He'd taken that account.

When Chelsea came around to congratulate him—begrudgingly, he noted—he'd given her a taste of her own medicine. "*Smoked* you," he said. "Bada-bing, bada-boom."

Chelsea had put her hands on her waist and glared up at him. "Nice," she'd said. "Exactly what I would expect of a guy who plays to the lowest denominator."

"What's that supposed to mean?"

"Figure it out," she'd said enigmatically as she tried to make an exit out of his cubicle. But Ian's wasn't as neat as hers, and his gym bag and basketball shoes were on the floor. She'd tripped on them and knocked into the wall, hitting her elbow. "*Ooouch*," she'd said with a painful wince as she stumbled out of his cubicle.

"Serves you right," he'd muttered.

Shortly after that, the Tesla account was dangled before him. Ian was definitely the man for it, and in fact, he wanted it so bad that he'd come up with three spots to show the partners, not just the one they'd asked for. His showpiece was the sex appeal with a conscience, but he also had a how-far-how-fast-can-you-go-on-a-charge spot and another one for the made-in-America spot. He wasn't going in with just one idea. He was going in with a *campaign*. A menu of genius for them to choose from, if you will.

Tomorrow was the pitch to the top dogs at the

agency, and on Friday, the partners would announce which campaign they were presenting to Tesla. The word on the street was that this account was Grabber-Paulson's to lose, so it was assumed in the office that whoever the partners chose would win the account management.

He didn't know exactly what Chelsea had planned, but he'd heard some talk around the office that led him to believe he had this in the bag. That hadn't stopped him from baiting her every chance he got, mainly because he never failed to get a reaction and secondly because he really wanted the Tesla account and was not above a little gamesmanship. It wouldn't hurt to knock his competition off balance. And he wasn't going to cut her a break just because she was a woman. He was going to win, and he was going to crush his competition on the way.

He worked that afternoon on some other accounts, and at about three o'clock, he thought he'd get some coffee. As he walked toward the break room, he happened to notice Chelsea inside one of the conference rooms. All of the conference rooms had glass walls, the theory being that just seeing people be creative would spark creativity. That's why there were so many big toys lying around too—basketball hoops, pogo sticks, big balls to roll around. Creativity went hand in hand with play, so they said. Ian never had any brilliant advertising ideas when he dropped in on a game of basketball near his apartment, but whatever. He supposed it worked for some.

Chelsea was pacing in front of a blank projection screen, talking. What she was doing, practicing her pitch? Ian changed direction and headed for the conference room, strolling in through the open door.

It took a moment for Chelsea to notice him, which gave Ian a moment to admire her. He was going to crush her tomorrow, but that didn't stop him from appreciating a figure that guys like him dreamed about. Chelsea was wearing a skirt today. It hit about mid-thigh and was tight enough to show off all her curves. She looked a bit taller today too. He glanced at her feet and noticed the shoes. Chelsea was walking on stilts, and her legs, good God, her *legs*. She was smoking hot in that dress and those shoes.

"Hey!" she said sharply, her voice full of accusation.

Ian's head snapped up. "Hey," he said congenially. "Practicing your pitch?" He settled one hip onto the conference table.

"Do you mind?" She gestured to the door in a be-off-with-you way.

."If you want, I could listen and give you some feedback."

Chelsea's mouth dropped open. And then her green eyes narrowed into little slits. "You have got to be the most arrogant man I've ever met."

Ian smiled and shrugged.

"You can go, Ian," she said, marching around the conference table to usher him out. "I think I've got it."

"Suit yourself."

"I *will*."

"So hostile," he said with a wink as he stood up. "I'm just trying to help. It never hurts for someone to hear the pitch, right? You've had someone listen to you go through it, right?"

"Yes, I've had—Hey, *hey*," she said, poking him in the chest. "Are you trying to play me?" she demanded. "Because it won't work. I'm not some junior account person, you know. You can't intimidate me."

"Well, obviously," Ian said and poked her back. "You wouldn't be pitching at all if you were a junior account person. I know I can't intimidate you. It wasn't a declaration of war, you know; it was an offer to help."

"It wasn't a let-me-help, best-friends-forever offer, either. I'm not playing games with you. This account means a lot to me—"

"Me too."

"Oh yeah?" she said, shifting closer. "Well, don't get too attached to the idea. I've got seniority, you know."

"So why are you so afraid to show me what you've got?"

"Because it's none of your business."

"On the eve of the championship, it's okay to go out and shoot some hoops with your competitor. It's not going to affect tomorrow's big game. It's not like I can go out and change weeks of work overnight if I see you've got something better."

She laughed. "Good try, Rafferty, but I think maybe the reason you want to see *my* pitch is because you're worried about the strength of *your* pitch. Is it a little rough? Maybe I should listen to you." She winked, and her green eyes shone with pleasure at her comeback.

"I'm definitely *not* worried about my pitch."

"No? Seems to me if you're presenting three," she said, holding up three fingers and wiggling them at him, "then you must be uncertain which one is the winner." Her smile broadened into sheer triumph, as if she thought she'd really zinged him.

She hadn't zinged him, but Ian did wonder how she knew what he had...*Zach*. Of course. That rat bastard. "Have you been talking to Zimmerman?" he asked accusingly.

She shrugged and studied her manicure. "Maybe. Does it matter? I thought we were doing the let's-help-each-other thing. But if we're not, would you mind toddling off? I have a lot of work I need to do before tomorrow. I plan to hit the ground running with this account on Monday."

She was amazingly and annoyingly confident. Ian was generally a confident guy, but she was making him a teensy bit nervous. "You really think you're going to get this, don't you?"

"I don't think, I *know*," she said, looking up.

He tilted his head to one side to study her. "Isn't it obvious to you why they brought me in?"

"I don't know—I haven't given it the slightest bit of thought." She lifted her chin, and Ian realized she lied about as well as she engaged in verbal volleyball. "I've been promised that this account is as good as mine. Didn't they tell you *that* when they brought you in?"

A bit more of Ian's confidence leaked out of him. He'd been in New York advertising long enough to know that the industry was full of snakes. He wouldn't put it past anyone to feed him a bunch of half-baked promises to get him to commit. "Who told you?"

She grinned. "None of your beeswax."

"Come on, tell me—" His phone rang, distracting him momentarily. He fished it out of his pocket and noticed the number was the Grabber-Paulson main number. That was weird. "Listen, I'll just say this," he said, clicking off the phone. "Don't be so sure of things. People say things they don't mean, especially in this industry." He started for the door.

"Uh-huh, I know. And I would offer you the same advice, Mr. Rafferty," she said in a singsong voice, and she flashed a dazzling smile, full of straight white teeth.

"Cocky too. I like that about you," he said. "I'll keep it in mind when I make partner." He winked at her, smiled as if he was completely unbothered, and went out of the conference room. He paused just outside the door and hit the button to return the phone call. Hadeetha, the receptionist, picked it up. "Hi, Hadeetha," Ian said. "Did someone call me from this number?"

"Hi, Ian," she said, her voice a little giggly. "Yes, you had a call. Just one moment." She cut over to another line before Ian could ask her who had called. It rang five times before hitting the message box. *"You've reached the voice mail of Brad Paulson..."*

Brad was the managing partner, and Ian's pulse ticked up a notch when he heard his voice. He left a message in Brad's box that he'd returned his call and then went back to his cubicle to ponder why Paulson would be calling him on the eve of the presentations. And in the midst of wondering, Ian was suddenly struck by the vision of Chelsea's sparkling green eyes. Was she *right*? Paulson could be calling about any of his accounts, but Ian quickly thought through them—there was nothing going on in any of them that would rise to the level of partner. Had Chelsea really been promised this account? Had they lured him over here only to give a big car account like Tesla to someone else? Why else would Paulson be calling him? It wasn't as if they were working together on any particular thing.

Ian couldn't concentrate with that hanging over his head, so he detoured and went by Paulson's office and caught his assistant as she was donning her coat.

"Oh hey," he said. "Is Brad around?"

"He's in a meeting." She glanced over her shoulder, and so did Ian, to the windows. The snow was really coming down.

"Could you please tell him I understand he's looking for me and that I dropped by?"

"Sure, I'll leave him a message. But I'm getting out of here before it gets too deep."

"Thanks," Ian said. "I appreciate it."

He went back to his desk. He could see Chelsea across the room, still in the conference room, still walking back and forth, reviewing her pitch.

Okay, Ian could at least admit to himself that he was a little worried now. It just seemed a little too coincidental that Chelsea was feeling so confident and the managing partner was trying to get in touch with him on the eve of the presentation. He decided to take a look at his pitch again.

Chapter 3

FARRAH STUCK HER HEAD IN THE CONFERENCE room door. "I'm going home. It's snowing."

If Chelsea hadn't been so laser focused on getting her pitch just right, she would have mentioned to Farrah that it snows a lot in New York and that most people didn't leave at three in the afternoon because of it. But she didn't have the energy or the patience to explain it this afternoon. "Okay. See you tomorrow."

"Yeah, if the trains are running." Farrah was also an eternal pessimist.

Chelsea looked toward the window and noticed the snow was coming down pretty thick. Great, just great. She didn't have boots with her, only a pair of raggedy tennis shoes. The right one had a hole forming in the big toe. She had the pumps she'd worn to work, but those were cheap and would not hold up in the snow. Why couldn't she remember to leave some boots at the office, for heaven's sake?

And speaking of shoes, an hour of wearing the insanely expensive ones she'd bought for the presentation had made her feet numb. She kicked them off and turned the page of her notes. She was ready. She'd reviewed her pitch many times and had practiced saying it all aloud. The best use of her time at this point was to review her ad once more and see if there were any last-minute refinements she could make in the pacing.

She left the conference room and noticed that the floor looked deserted. She could see Caden Trent, his head bent over a light board. Sarah Fedrovsky was still at work too, probably on her new paper products account. Across the floor, the light in Jason's office was on, and Chelsea assumed he was there, tossing that damn Nerf ball around. Just outside his door was Ian Rafferty's cubicle. It seemed like every time she'd walked by Ian's cubicle in the last few months, he was leaning back in his chair, his suit jacket off, his tie loosened at the throat. He generally had one leg propped up on his desk and was gabbing away into the telephone. It didn't seem to Chelsea that Ian worked as much as he talked.

The other thing Chelsea had noticed about his

cubicle—in addition to the papers and books and sports bags everywhere—was the award on his desk. It was a flying magazine in bronze, won for some print campaign. Yeah, well, it wasn't a Clio, which was what Chelsea was after. She was determined to win one and put it in her new corner office.

Chelsea moved on to the media room and queued up her ad.

Good-looking man with silver-streaked hair and a woman with fashionable gray hair and equally attractive come out of a restaurant and wait for the valet to bring their car around. It's a Tesla. They drive off into a starry night. Camera cuts to images of their life—grandkid's car seat in back, tennis rackets, a ski pass hanging from the rearview. They drive up the Pacific Coast Highway, talking and laughing. An approaching car swerves around behind a truck; driver reacts quickly and veers out of the path. Woman looks back, her hand on the man's arm. They exchange a look, a shared lifetime flashing before their eyes. Camera pans out, Tesla zipping down the highway. Tesla: Superb handling. Because you expect it.

It was a good ad, a *great* ad, and Chelsea was excited about presenting it. But she thought that the ad could use a tiny bit of tightening in the middle and spent a bit of time with that until she was satisfied it was perfect. And because she believed no one could overprepare, she ran through her presentation and ad one last time.

It was rock solid, and Chelsea smiled to herself, very happy with her work. She would definitely get this account; there was no question in her mind. She'd done everything she could possibly do to prepare. There was nothing else she could do to improve it—it was the perfect ad for a perfect car.

She'd lost two out of three accounts to Ian in the last few months, but that was not enough to pull her spirits down. Jason had told her this was her account. No one could argue that her idea didn't hit the sweet spot of advertising. How could they *not* give it to her?

Full of optimism, she fairly bounced out of the media room, surprised to find the floor almost completely deserted at only four o'clock. The only lights she could see were coming from Ian's cubicle and from Sarah's.

Had everyone bailed because of the snow? Chelsea wondered if maybe she should head home too.

In her cubicle, Chelsea gathered her things, taking care to include everything she would need to prepare for tomorrow. Attention to detail, in her mind, was what had made her successful in this business. By the end of next week, maybe she would be in the empty corner office that overlooked Gramercy Park. Well. Not *overlooked* it, exactly, but if you stood in the corner and leaned right, you could see the edge of the park. And you didn't see the CVS on the corner at all.

Okay, maybe the vacant corner office didn't have much of a view, but it was an *office*. It had a door, and the door could be closed, and quiet could reign. She could talk on the phone without Farrah overhearing everything she said. She could *think*. The raise Chelsea would get was great, but that office…that was the best part of the whole thing.

Chelsea pulled on her old tennis shoes and stuffed her Manolos into her tote bag in the allotted shoe spots. She donned a jacket, a car coat over that, and then a raincoat over that. Next came her earmuffs and the hat with the orange fluff ball on top—not exactly the chicest thing Chelsea owned, but definitely the warmest. Last, but certainly not least, she had her mittens in hand. She managed to wedge her tote over her arm and onto her shoulder and started for the elevator.

She stopped by to say good night to Sarah, but Sarah was gone. She'd forgotten to turn off her light. Chelsea did it for her. Now, the only light was Ian's. She made a slight detour to go around to his cubicle.

"Oh," she said, mildly surprised to see he was still in the office when she stuck her head around the wall.

Ian started. "Hi." He took in her outerwear, tapping a pen against a blank legal notepad. He looked up at her hat and the orange ball and said something. Chelsea was fairly certain he said *nice hat*, but with her hat and earmuffs, it was a little hard to tell.

She pushed back her earmuffs. "So, everyone took off a little early, huh?"

"Looks like it," he said. "The snow's gotten pretty bad."

"Aren't you going home?"

"Not yet." He tossed the pen down and stretched his arms high before folding them over his chest. "I've got a few things I want to do first."

Chelsea couldn't resist. "You look a little anxious. Maybe I can help you punch it up. Your pitch, I mean. You're worried about your pitch, right?"

A slow smile of amusement moved across Ian's face. "Thanks...but I'm not sure you can offer anything that could improve what I've got. It's solid."

"Wow. No improvement possible. That must be some pitch."

"I didn't say it was impossible to improve it. I said it was impossible for *you* to improve it."

Chelsea laughed. She tried to fold her arms. But given the number of pieces of outerwear she was wearing, her arms bounced back to her side. "Just for clarification, which pitch is it that doesn't need improvement? I mean, out of the three."

Ian's smile broadened, and when it did, his blue eyes sparked, putting Chelsea back on her heels a bit. The man had a very nice smile, which, if she were being honest, she would admit that she had noticed before today. Many times, actually. But up close and directed at her, it made him look… super hot. Hot enough to maybe torch a few things. Build a fire. Flambé a decadent dessert. Scorch an entire forest.

"If you'd like, I could teach you how to come up with three complementing ads after I land this account."

"Oh…you wish," Chelsea said, and she snorted. When she did, her tote bag slid right off her arm and hit the floor.

Ian instantly moved to pick it up. He stood up, straightening to his full height, all six feet two of him. He was so close to her that she could see that the spark in his eye went much deeper than she'd ever noticed before this very moment. "You know what I wish, Chelsea?" he asked, his voice low and smooth, his eyes mesmerizing.

Chelsea could not help her gaze sliding to his mouth, and she dumbly shook her head.

He leaned closer still and took her hand in his. "I wish you the best of luck tomorrow." He slipped the handles of her tote over her hand and then up her arm to her shoulder, wedging it on there, and then leaned closer—so close that for one mad, heart-fluttering moment, Chelsea thought he was actually going to kiss her. "*Because you're going to need it.*"

He faded back. Chelsea was momentarily speechless. He had just used his über sex appeal to zing her. Her eyes narrowed accusingly. "Oh, I won't need it. But *you* will, buster." *Ha*.

Ian grinned a little lopsidedly, and his eyes, good Lord, his eyes radiated sex. "You sure about that?"

Something warm and fluid snaked down Chelsea's spine. She could feel the pull of his orbit, and she could imagine how many times he had used that sloe-eyed look to lure women to him. She stepped back, out of the gravitational force field around him. "I'm *very* sure. This is some of my best work. And I didn't need three ads to nail it."

One of his brows arched higher than the other. "You know, that can be a turnoff for some guys. But for me? That cocky overconfidence is a definite turn-on. Want to come over to my place?"

"I am *not* overcon—" She suddenly realized what he was doing. "That," she said, twirling a finger at him, "will not work on me."

Ian propped his arm on top of his cubicle wall. "Seriously, Crawford, your smack talk could use some work. I'd be happy to help you with it."

She took another step back. "News flash—in about eighteen hours from now, I won't need to work on anything but this account. Play your cards right, and maybe I'll bring you along to work on it with me." She smiled, pleased with herself for that one.

And then she bumped into his cubicle wall. *Again.*

Ian chuckled.

Chelsea straightened herself, readjusted her tote bag, and with a jaunty two-fingered wave, she went out of the office, rolling her eyes at her inability to successfully engage in a bit of baiting.

Or make a powerful exit.

She had no trouble getting an elevator and, in fact, was the only one aboard for the thirty-one-story plunge. When the doors opened on to the lobby, she was surprised to see only the security guard. He was at his desk, a small TV blaring just beneath the counter. He was buttoning up a down jacket. "Hope you can get to where you're going. The mayor is advising everyone to shelter in place."

"What? You're kidding," Chelsea said. On the security guard's little TV, she could see a swath of blue across the entire East Coast. She hurried to the front of the building to peer down the street toward the subway. The snow was so thick she couldn't see it. The coming and going from the building had created a path, and the mounds of snow on either side looked a foot high.

"How is that possible?" she said to the security guard. "It was hardly even snowing at lunch."

"Big storm," he said. "Snowpocalypse they're calling it. Supposed to dump another foot tonight." He shut off his television and turned the collar of his coat up. "It's climate change, you know. When I was a kid, we never had snow like this, not this late in the season."

Chelsea didn't care about climate change in that moment—she cared about how cold her feet were going to be by the time she got home. She wondered how quickly one contracted frostbite.

The security guard walked with her to the door. "Have a good one," he said, and he went out, walking in the opposite direction of the subway and quickly disappearing into the blizzard.

Chelsea adjusted her tote bag on her shoulder, pulled her hat low over her eyes, and went out, trudging in the direction of the subway.

That train was going to be stuffed like a burrito.

Chapter 4

Ian had been playing phone tag with Brad. He'd made the crucial mistake of stepping into the men's room, and in those few minutes, Brad had packed up and left with the mad exodus of staff. But Brad had left a message on Ian's cell phone asking him to call. Of course Ian had called him immediately—but it rolled to voice mail.

Whatever it was that Brad wanted would wait, Ian decided. He was the only one left in the office, and judging by the snow he could see coming down outside Jason's windows, he ought to get out of here too.

Ian shoved his last-minute notes into his bag, wordlessly chiding himself for allowing Chelsea to ruffle him this afternoon. That wasn't like him—Ian loved a good challenge, loved being the underdog. He thrived on competition, and in fact, he'd started it with her. But he'd left a partner track to come to this job, lured away by good money and a promise of quick, upward mobility. He'd left everything he'd worked hard to achieve at Huntson-Jones, because Grabber-Paulson was offering him the same thing, only faster. But it all hinged on getting the plum accounts, like this one. And he realized, too late, that he wasn't as sure of his decision as he had thought.

The truth was that Ian had liked Huntson-Jones. But in the end, he thought taking the leap was what he was supposed to do after all the years spent building a reputation.

His friends had told him to leap too. "They don't offer that salary because they want to test you out," Ben had said. "What are you waiting for?" Devin had asked him, and both had good-naturedly shoved him out the door.

Frankly, Ian didn't know what he was waiting for, but it felt like he was always *waiting*. Maybe he'd been waiting for this very opportunity. Maybe he needed to give it more than a few months before he came to any conclusions. He only knew that since he'd done the thing he thought he ought to do, the thing that seemed to make the most sense, he'd had a few second thoughts.

Today, he'd let those second thoughts turn into doubts and get the best of him.

"Too late for doubts, man," he muttered. He was all in, ready to rock and roll. He reverted back to his standard pep talk: first the Tesla account and then, who knew? The sky was the limit, right?

Right.

But why did he sometimes feel as if maybe the sky was the wrong thing to aim for? Maybe he ought to be aiming for the horizon or a totally new challenge—

His phone rang. Ian almost killed himself getting it out of his pocket. "Hello," he said, trying not to sound antsy.

"Ian, are you believing this weather?" Brad shouted into the phone, the wind carrying his words away from the receiver.

"I haven't made it out yet." Ian realized he was shouting too.

"You should get out of there! It's *crazy* out here—I've never seen so much snow! It's hell, only white. White hell. So look, I've got some good news for you, Ian. Me, all the partners—we like you. We like the way you think and the way you present. Jason's had a chance to look at the work you and Chelsea have done, the partners have done some talking, and we're giving you the account."

Ian was shocked. Of all the things he thought Brad might say, this was not it. It was great news,

great news. It confirmed everything he'd believed
about himself. So why should an image of the
woman bundled up like an Arctic ice fisherman
who'd just left the office pop into his head? Why
should he be concerned with how hard Chelsea
had worked for this?

"Hello? Are you there?" Brad shouted.

"Yes, yes, I'm here!" Ian said, shaking it off.

"I thought you'd be happy!"

"I am!" Ian said, recovering quickly. "Thank
you! I won't let you down, Brad. I'm just…" He
ran his hand over his head. "*Surprised*. What about
the pitches?"

"Right, right, the timing is no good on that.
We made the decision just this afternoon, because
we've only got a week to get ready for the final
presentations to Tesla. We're going to go ahead
with the pitch tomorrow," Brad said. "We know
how hard Chelsea has worked and it's only fair
that she get her chance to present."

It seemed patently *un*-fair to Ian for them to
hear her pitch, knowing they would not give her
the account.

"It's good for the office to do these things,"
Brad said, sounding as if he had prepared himself
for an argument. "Good practice for partnerships.
In your case, it will be great practice for the pitch

to Tesla next week. Be ready to go; present like you don't have the account. And congratulations, Ian! Great work!"

"Thanks," Ian said. "Thanks for the opportunity."

"We're expecting big things from you, you know—*big* things! This is your chance to wow us. Now get out of the office! It's too nasty to be holed up there!"

"I will," Ian said. "I'm leaving now." He wished Brad an easy trip home, then clicked off.

He didn't move, just stood rooted to the floor. He was thrilled. Of course he was thrilled. This was exactly what he'd come to Grabber-Paulson to do. This is what he'd worried about all afternoon, that he *wouldn't* get the account. So why wasn't he doing his happy dance?

Ian tossed his phone onto his desk, put his hands on his hips, and looked to his left, to where the Director of Media—the fancy title this account carried—would be housed. A corner office with actual sunlight filtering into it. Ian didn't like the way the firm had handled this, but hey, he would have won the account anyway. And he felt great about his work.

Still—what had just happened to Chelsea sucked. She didn't get a chance. That she didn't even know left a very bad taste in his mouth. He thought about her walking around that conference room, honing her pitch. He knew how hard she'd worked—everyone on the floor knew how hard she'd worked.

He picked up his bag.

Chelsea would bounce back. This business was cutthroat, and if you couldn't bounce back, you had no business being here. Chelsea would accept it and move on to the next account.

Ian checked his watch, wondering if he could rouse Ben and Devin for a celebratory beer. He donned his coat and wound his scarf around his neck. He picked up his bag and shoved his hands in his coat pockets, looking for his gloves and his knit hat as he strolled around the cubicles toward the entrance. The lights flickered; he glanced up, wondering what was going on. He heard the slam of the stairwell door and figured it was the security guard. But just as he rounded the corner and stepped into the reception area, the office doors suddenly banged open, and Chelsea waddled in, collapsed against the door, and then doubled over, dragging air into her lungs.

"Chelsea! What's wrong?" he exclaimed and rushed to her side, putting his hand on her back and leaning over her.

"*Snow. Pocalypse*," she said through drags of

air, and she slid down the door to her bottom. "The trains aren't running because of some massive power outage. The elevators aren't working, either. *We are on the thirty-first floor*," she said through a wheeze.

"You walked up thirty-one floors?"

She shook her head. "I took the elevator to twenty. I stopped to hit the vending machines and they stopped working then. I could have been stuck in the elevator. Ohmigod, I would have been *stuck* in the *elevator*." She started pulling candy bars out of her coat pocket and throwing them on the floor. She suddenly stopped and looked up at him with big green eyes. "Oh no. No, no, *no*! I can't be stuck in here with *you*!"

"With me!" he said, surprised. "Why not? Maybe I can't be stuck in here with you!"

She groaned and closed her eyes. Ian looked at Chelsea, the small mound of candy, and the door as reality began to seep into that reception area. *No*. No, hell no, he couldn't be stuck in here with her, not knowing what he knew now. He couldn't bear it, couldn't stand the thought of her trying to one-up him. He suddenly darted out the office suite doors to the elevator banks and banged the down button. There was no light, nothing.

"You know, if the power goes off, these doors

lock," Chelsea said. Ian glanced over his shoulder. She was still on the floor but had leaned over to push the door open. "It's a security thing." She removed her hand, and the glass door closed.

Ian hit the elevator button again. But as he did, her words penetrated his thoughts. Ian turned back to look at her. Chelsea was on her back now, her arms spread wide, still sucking wind. He had never seen her like that, and he meant to say so, but the lights flickered overhead. Ian had a vision of being locked outside the office and in the elevator bank. He dove for the office door, crashing into it in his haste to open it before it locked. He tripped, falling just beside Chelsea as the door slid to a close and the locks clicked shut.

The lights went out.

He shifted, wanting to stand, but his hand hit something gooshy.

"Hey!" Chelsea said.

"Sorry." Apparently the gooshy thing was her.

"Surely there is a gen—"

Lights along the wall sputtered to life, casting a dull gray light. Ian looked down; he'd landed on a package of peanut butter and chocolate, and it had smeared his trouser leg.

Chelsea was sitting up. He hopped to his feet and walked to the glass doors, pulling hard against them. They would not budge. He held his ID card up to the card reader.

"You have to have a key."

"Yeah, well, I don't have a key."

Chelsea rolled over and pushed herself up onto her feet. She unzipped her coat and removed it. Then she removed a coat under that and then the jacket under *that*. She unwrapped her scarf and let it drop, pulled off her hat and ear muffs, pushed her hair out of her face, and bent over, stiff legged, to rummage through her bag. When she stood again, she proudly held out a key. "Ta-da! You get one of these when you become an account manager." She gave him a pert little smile and handed him the key.

Ian looked at the key and then at her. "You knew you had a key and yet you let me think I would be locked out?"

She smiled and shrugged a little.

"I almost killed myself," he said, pointing to the chocolate stain on his trousers.

"Please. I would never be that lucky." She smiled again.

If it hadn't been for that smile, he might have strangled her. He gave her a look before stalking to the door, put the key in the lock, and tried to turn it. It wouldn't budge. He jiggled it around. Nothing. "This doesn't work."

"What do you mean it doesn't work?" she said anxiously, and she was suddenly beside him, jostling him out of the way. The key wouldn't turn for her, either.

Chelsea yanked it out and held it up to the dim light. "Oh *no!*"

"What?"

"This is my spare apartment key!"

"Okay, well, look into your bag and get the right one," he said, gesturing to her tote bag, from which one shoe was protruding.

"No, no, it's not there," she said frantically. "I have the wrong key in my purse, Ian! How can I have the wrong key? I'll tell you how," she said before he could answer. "I have a bowl at home where I keep all my keys. I must have picked up this one by mistake."

He wondered how many keys the woman had that she required a bowl, but never mind that—"Are you telling me we are really locked in?"

She looked up at the ceiling lights. "At least until the power comes on again."

"*Aaaah!*" Ian said and kicked the door in frustration. "That could be hours!"

Chelsea gasped. "*Hours!*" She suddenly whirled around and picked up a chair, one that was next to the receptionist's desk for visitors. She tried to raise it over her head for reasons that first eluded Ian, but then she hoisted it against her chest, legs out, and started for the door.

"Whoa, whoa," he said, grabbing her around the waist and hauling her into his chest to stop her from ramming the chair through the door. "What are you doing?" he exclaimed as he wrested the chair from her grip.

"Breaking us out!" she cried. "I can't be here all night! I have to get some sleep. I have to be ready for tomorrow!"

A twinge of guilt nicked him. "First of all, that's tempered glass, Chelsea. You'd just knock yourself out. Second, I don't think the partners would be too happy to find you busted out like that because you need your beauty rest."

She gasped as if he'd just slapped her. "What a sexist thing to say! It's not beauty rest; it's just *rest*."

"You're missing the point—okay fine," Ian retorted, in no mood to debate her. "You don't need beauty rest, obviously."

She blinked at him. And then she seemed to actually blush a little, although it was hard to tell as low as the light was. And then she sagged against him, giving up. "I'm just saying—we have to get out."

"We'll get out," he said, and he gave her a reassuring pat on the shoulder that he didn't quite feel. She wasn't the only one who needed her beauty sleep. Correction—he needed beauty sleep. She just needed sleep.

He remembered that Jason had a television in his office and began striding in that direction.

"Wait, where are you going? Do you know another way out?" Chelsea asked.

Ian didn't respond, just kept walking. He could hear her run to catch up to him.

He walked into Jason's office and turned on the TV. The meteorologist was gesturing to a huge swath of blue that covered the entire east coast. Chelsea crowded in beside him—actually, she gave him a bit of a shove out of the way so she could stand in front of the TV. He gently nudged her to one side. They stood, shoulder to shoulder, watching.

"This is one for the ages, folks. If you haven't heard, the mayor is advising everyone to shelter in place," the weatherman said. "Now, back to Debbie and any news on the power outages."

"Oh my God," Ian groaned.

"I don't think anyone will have much choice about sheltering in place, Frank," Debbie said. She was standing somewhere in the city, the snow swirling around her. Emergency generator lights were shining on crews working behind her. "The power outages in the city have affected all travel. Very few lines are running, and as you can see," she said, turning to gesture to the crews behind her, "there is a lot of work going on in this terrible cold and wind to get the power back on. Snowdrifts are affecting the subway and train schedules as well. We have lists of all the delays and outages on our website. Unfortunately, more snow keeps falling and with no end in sight."

"It's a snowpocalypse out there, folks," said the newscaster in the studio. "Stay where you are. Heed the mayor's warning to shelter in place. The snow is falling so fast the city is struggling to keep up with clearing the roads. Frank, when will we be out of the woods?" he asked, throwing it back to the meteorologist.

"By morning this massive system will have moved out over the Atlantic," Frank said, his hands swirling around the Atlantic. "Let me show you why we got so much more snow than we were expecting—"

"This can't be happening," Ian muttered and he clicked off the TV.

"Oh. My. *God*," Chelsea said. She picked up the Nerf basketball from Jason's desk and threw it as hard as she could. It floated over the hoop and wafted to the floor.

The lights flickered. Ian and Chelsea looked at each other just as the lights went out.

"What just happened?" Chelsea exclaimed loudly. "I thought the generator was running!"

"It was," Ian said, looking curiously up at the lights.

"This is a nightmare!" Chelsea cried, and she whirled around to Jason's window, bracing her hands against it. Across the street, visible through the curtain of snow, was light in the windows of an office building. She whimpered and dropped her forehead against the glass.

Ian sighed. He shifted forward and put his arm around her shoulders. "Don't freak out," he said soothingly, giving her a little squeeze. "It's going to be okay."

"Ohmigod. I am not freaking out, Ian. Why do you think I am freaking out? Do you honestly think all women need beauty rest and freak out at the first sign of adversity?"

"What is the matter with you?" he demanded. "You look like you're about to cry. If that's not freaking out, what is?"

"I'm not going to *cry*. And even if I was, it's just crying. It's another way to release tension. Sort of like meditation, only uglier."

The generator's lights suddenly flickered back on, washing them in dishwater-gray light once more.

"Thank heavens," she said, and she pushed past him. He watched her march for the door of the office.

"Okay, where are *you* going?" he asked.

"To find something to eat! I'm starving!"

So was he, come to think of it, and he followed her.

Chelsea marched to the break room. She walked up to the fridge and yanked open the door. Her face instantly fell and she covered her mouth with her hand. "That is so *disgusting*," she said.

Ian moved and dipped to see over her shoulder. There were old fast food containers and some food in plastic containers—in one, he could see the mold that was growing inside. Food had been spilled on the fridge shelves. He watched as Chelsea reached for a can of tomato juice and tried to dislodge it from whatever had congealed around it. She couldn't.

"Oh God—shut that thing," Ian said, covering his nose with his hand.

She abruptly stepped back as she slammed the fridge door shut and stepped on his foot.

"Ouch," Ian said.

"Sorry." She looked around the break room. "I have to eat something or I will pass out. Oh, I know! Ron Early always has some food in his desk." She started out of the break room.

She was right—Ian had seen a loaf of bread on Ron's shelves. He had some food account that was always sending over samples.

Chelsea walked into Ron's cubicle and made a sound of delight at seeing the bread on top of his bookshelves. "Eureka!" she said. "There has to be some peanut butter here."

"Wait," Ian said, and he took the loaf of bread from her. He pointed to the signs of mold through the packaging, barely visible in the dim light.

Chelsea squinted at it. "*No*," she groaned. "Okay, we'll just tear the bits of mold off—"

"I've got a better idea," Ian said. He thought he could help—he thought he *needed* to help, or this was going to be a very long night. "Will you promise to chill out a little if I show you where some food is? And I'm not talking candy bars from the vending machines or moldy bread. I'm talking *real* food."

"What kind of food?" she asked suspiciously.

"Lean Cuisine."

Chelsea's eyes sparked with delight. "Really?" she asked, her hand going to her belly. "You'd better not be kidding me right now, Ian Rafferty. Because if you are kidding me, I will karate chop you in the neck. I am starving."

He laughed. "I'm not kidding. I know where there is a virtual cornucopia of Lean Cuisines."

That actually earned a smile from Chelsea. A sparkly, happy smile that struck Ian as unusually pretty. "Then we have a deal."

Chapter 5

CHELSEA FOLLOWED IAN ACROSS THE SUITE AND down a corridor to the partners' offices. He walked right into Brad Paulson's office as if it were his and went around the desk and through a door. Chelsea hesitated before stepping across the threshold. She wasn't exactly comfortable with the idea of walking into the office of the man who would probably decide her fate tomorrow.

She paused to look around at Brad's office. She'd been in here three, maybe four times. Through the big plate-glass windows, she could see that night had fallen, and the snow was a lacy curtain between their offices and the world. It looked entirely staged, like a Christmas ad where the family comes trooping home in the midst of a holiday snowfall, dragging a tree behind them, ready for their cocoa.

Ian's head popped out from the door. "Are you coming?"

"We shouldn't be in here," she whispered loudly.

"We shouldn't be stuck inside these offices without a key, either." His head disappeared.

Chelsea walked deeper into the office and looked around at the contemporary furnishings, the shelf with the various awards, the large, flat screen TV on one wall. There was a small conference table surrounded by thick leather chairs. Brad's desk was oversized, and with the exception of a few files neatly stacked in one corner, it was clean.

This was exactly how Chelsea pictured her new office would look. A bit smaller, of course. And with a few touches to make it a little warmer. Maybe some flower arrangements. And definitely a more casual desk—

"Tuscan chicken or vegetable lasagna?" Ian called out.

Food. Chelsea darted across Brad's office, careful not to put her tennis shoes on his rugs, and peeked in the door Ian had gone through. She was surprised to see a kitchenette. The few times she'd been in Brad's office, she'd assumed this door led to a bathroom. There was a bathroom—she could see the sink through a door at the other end of the room. But fifteen feet from that, on the other side of some cabinets and counters that looked as if they were used for storage, there was a kitchen-ette with a small fridge, a sink and cabinets, and a microwave.

"Wow. He could live in here," she said in wonder.

"Yep," Ian said as he reached into one of the cabinets and pulled out some plates.

"How did you know this kitchen was here?" Chelsea asked.

"Hanging around to talk to Brad when he was working late."

Did he mean hanging around to run his ideas past Brad? To find out which ones resonated with him? Chelsea could kick herself—she'd never thought to do that.

Ian held out the cartons of Lean Cuisines to her. "Which do you want?"

"Ian!" Chelsea said, and she looked over her shoulder, half expecting Brad to come striding through the door at any moment. "We can't take his food!"

"I'll take the lasagna," Ian said. "And I don't think Brad is going to be too upset, seeing as we are locked in. If you're worried about it, I'll talk to him—"

"No, nope. No need for that," she said quickly. She could imagine how that conversation would go. Ian would say something like *Chelsea was concerned she shouldn't be rummaging through your things* and fail to mention he'd been the first one in.

Ian smiled, almost as if he could read her thoughts. "Hey, I'd cover for you. I'm a nice guy that way." He offered her the Tuscan chicken.

Chelsea took the box from his hand and tore it open. "I didn't know you were so chummy with Brad."

"I wouldn't call it *chummy*, exactly."

"So what would you call it?" she asked, shifting her gaze to the box. "Buttering him up? Picking his brain? Getting an advantage on the Tesla account?" She stuck the container in the microwave and punched the buttons without thinking, as she happened to be on intimate terms with a diet of Lean Cuisine.

"Well, I could have," Ian happily admitted. "But the truth is I was just being a guy. Guys talk, Chelsea." He reached around her, his chest—a very hard chest—brushing against her back in that tiny kitchenette, and grabbed some forks.

"Sure, that's all it was."

"What, you don't believe me? As it turns out, there are several big Knicks fans in this office, myself and Brad included in that number."

"Hey!" She turned around, her shoulder

bumping into his chest. "*I* like the Knicks," she said defensively.

"You *do*?"

"You don't have to look so surprised."

"Well, I am," he said. "I never would have guessed you for a Knicks fan."

"Why not?" Chelsea demanded.

"Chelsea, calm down," he said with a smile. "I just mean that you don't have any Knicks paraphernalia hanging around. You never mention it."

"That's because I usually have too much work to do to sit around and talk about last night's game. And how was I supposed to know the entire office was sitting around in Brad's office talking about the Knicks? No one told me."

"The entire office? I never said the entire office. I said *I* was. And I never mentioned it to you because you are clearly…you know." He stuffed his hands in his pocket and shrugged.

"No, I don't know. I am clearly…what?"

"Come on, you know what I mean," he said, and he gave her a small, slightly pathetic smile.

"No, I *don't* know what you mean."

"All right," he said as the microwave dinged. "I didn't tell you because you're a little uptight, all right? You don't exactly invite conversation."

Chelsea gasped. She closed her eyes with a

groan and dipped down with a bit of frustration, because it wasn't the first time she'd heard that. Her best friend, Angie, had told her the same thing one night after they'd been out at a bar. *There's, like, these don't-talk-to-me waves rolling off you.*

"Why does everyone keep *saying* that?" Chelsea took the container from the oven and dropped it onto a plate Ian held up to her. "I am *not* uptight," she said, as if that were a completely unreasonable thing to say, as if she were the poster child for free and easy, as if Farrah had not said, just two days ago, *You don't have to be so uptight about it* concerning something Chelsea didn't even recall now. "*Yes*, I have a good work ethic," she said, picking up the next box and ripping it open. "*Yes*, I put in long hours. But I have to—I have a lot of work. And anyway, what is wrong with being professional? You have to stir that," she said, motioning to the Lean Cuisine that she'd taken from the microwave.

"There is nothing wrong with being professional," Ian said, following her instructions. "But sometimes, you have to let your hair down too. Be a guy."

She paused in what she was doing and gave him a look. "You're kidding, right?"

"Nope," he said unapologetically. "It's a tough

ONE MAD NIGHT 65

industry. I'm just saying sometimes you have to play."

"I play," she said, but she frowned as she put the second entrée into the microwave. She wasn't sure she really knew what that meant. She could just picture Brad and Ian hanging out on the weekends. Was Brad married? She didn't know if he was. Maybe Brad's wife had taken an interest in Ian's bachelor status. Maybe she was inviting him to dinner parties with socialites—

"Just some friendly advice," Ian said, misreading her silence for disagreement. "You're moving in a man's world, Chelsea. Might as well adopt some of their habits."

"That is so ridiculous," she said, although she wasn't certain if it was, at least not in the world of advertising. She had noticed that women in advertising were often called aggressive and bossy, whereas men were go-getters and creative. "Would you adopt the habits of women if you were moving in an industry dominated by them?"

"Well now, that depends on what you'd advise," Ian said as he filled two glasses with tap water.

"I would *never* advise you to adopt habits that weren't yours already."

"Oh," he said, his eyes sparkling with amusement. "A bit above it, are you?" He winked at her and picked up the plate with the Tuscan chicken and the two glasses of water. He leaned forward, his gaze locked on hers. "See? *Uptight*." He strolled out of the kitchen.

"Professional!" she shouted back at him.

The microwave dinged. Chelsea removed the second entrée and put it on the plate, grabbed the two forks Ian had found, and followed him out to the small conference table.

"Here's the thing with you, Crawford," Ian said easily as he offered her a seat as if they were at a fine dining restaurant. "You treat me like an adversary when I could be your friend. You and I could *both* have been sitting around this very table eating Lean Cuisine with Brad."

The wound was just getting deeper. "He actually served you his *Lean Cuisine*?" she asked, feeling small.

"What? No," Ian said, looking at her as if that was preposterous. "I'm just saying, if we worked together, we—"

"I'm going to stop you right there," Chelsea said instantly. "I don't buy into that whole work together theory. We are in competition for a job. Plus, you're pals with Zimmerman, so naturally, I can't but help call your character into question." She arched a dark brow, challenging him to disagree. She meant it sincerely—there wasn't a greasier person than Zach Zimmerman in all of New York.

Ian laughed. "I stand by my earlier statement. You don't have to take this competition so seriously. But I will concede that you have a valid point about Zimmerman. I'll be right back."

He disappeared into the kitchen again. Chelsea looked at her Tuscan chicken and smiled. If he could agree with her that Zimmerman was sleazy, maybe he wasn't all bad.

Ian returned a moment later with a scented candle, the type that usually sat on the back of a toilet. "It's a little dark," he explained and set it on the table.

"Romantic," Chelsea said with an approving nod. "Pine mist too. I can almost believe we're in the middle of a forest."

"You know what they say, presentation is ninety percent of the battle." He picked up his fork and began to eat.

Chelsea watched him a minute. Did Ian have to be so damned good-looking on top of being so good at advertising and, apparently, at interpersonal relationships?

She looked down at her container, wishing she'd think of something else. "I can't believe we are sitting here dining by candlelight on the food we stole from the managing partners' fridge. If we ever get the Lean Cuisine account, I am totally using this in an ad," she said. "Lean Cuisine— perfect in a disaster."

Ian cast another gorgeous smile in her direction. "That's good. I'd bite," he said. "So…have you always been in advertising?"

"Yes—first job out of college. I applied on a lark and got the job. I was shocked."

"Did you get a degree in marketing?" he asked.

Chelsea laughed. "Nope. My degree is in English. I wanted to be a writer. I used to fill up notebooks with stories I thought I'd publish someday."

"Oh yeah? Have you published anything?"

Chelsea laughed again. "No. I *want* to write a book. But I haven't managed more than about twenty pages of a novel. It's not as easy as it looks, you know." She paused for a moment. "I still want to be a writer someday."

"It's hard to make a living as a writer," Ian pointed out.

"So I hear," Chelsea agreed.

"I like writing too."

"You do? You don't seem the type."

"Now who is being annoying?" he asked cheerfully.

Chelsea smiled. "Touché." She was beginning to see past God's gift to advertising. Ian was seeming more and more a very likable man. "So why did you come here, really?" she asked curiously.

"Where?"

"To Grabber-Paulson. I heard you were the best thing going at Huntson-Jones."

"Be still my heart," Ian said. "Chelsea Crawford just paid me a compliment."

"Don't blow it," she teased him. "I'm only starting to warm up to you."

"No way am I going to blow it," Ian said. "We might be stuck in here a while and the way you're attacking that Lean Cuisine, we could be fighting for them later."

"So?" she prodded, swirling her fork at him. "Why'd you come?"

"Well, for whatever reason, Grabber-Paulson came knocking. Jason called me and invited me to drinks. He and Brad said they had some great talent in-house but wanted more."

This, Chelsea noticed, he said while looking at his little tray of food.

"They talked to me about a fast track to partner, and they offered me a lot of money." He glanced up at her as he ate a bite of lasagna. "It was almost a no-brainer."

Chelsea could feel the blood rushing from her face. *A fast track to partner? A lot of money?* Why had Jason even called him? He'd told her they were so happy with her work. She could suddenly see Jason Sung's smiling face dancing before her eyes, and she really wanted to kick something. Hard. Instead she dropped her fork, gaining Ian's attention again. "Are you just saying that to rattle me? Is this some sort of game day strategy?"

"Not at all," he said, smiling curiously at her. "You asked. I told you."

Chelsea couldn't work it out. She couldn't understand why Brad and Jason would bring in someone new.

"What?" he asked, and she realized she was still staring at him.

"A lot of money," she repeated. "Do you mean a *lot* a lot or just a lot?"

He chuckled with bewilderment. "I don't know exactly what you mean, but I guess it's relative. It was a lot of money to me."

She was dying to ask him how much, but not only was that incredibly rude, she feared it might cause her to fling herself out a thirty-first-floor window. She sagged against her chair. How could they betray her like this? "I don't get it. I have worked my ass off for this firm and they haven't offered *me* a lot of money. They told me this account was mine, that I was due, and then the next thing I know, they're bringing in some hotshot from another firm," she said, gesturing at him.

"Thank you. I think."

"What is it?" she asked, casting her arms wide. "Is it because I'm a woman? It's because I'm a woman, isn't it? You said it, Ian; this is a good ol' boys club—"

"Hey, I did *not* say that—"

But Chelsea wasn't listening to him. She knew exactly what was going on here. She'd seen it with Candice Fletcher. Candice had worked at this firm for years and had done some of the best work Chelsea had seen. And she'd left last year, tired of bumping up against the glass ceiling, tired of working circles around men only to be passed over time and again. "It's the good ol' boys club, and they can't deal with a woman who might be smart or capable. They want us all to wear tight skirts and say yes sir, no sir, do you take cream with that coffee?"

"Hey," Ian said, and he put his hand on her arm. "I think you're overreacting—"

"Then explain to me why Jason would tell me this gig was mine and then offer you a *lot* of money and not me? There has to be *some* reason, right? I don't think it's my work because everyone says my work is great. It's not my work, is it? So what else can it be, Ian? I think it's because I'm a woman, and I'm not in here eating Lean Cuisine and talking about the Knicks!"

"Chelsea." Ian squeezed her arm. "It had nothing to do with the fact that you're a woman."

"What?" Her gaze suddenly riveted on him. The way he said it gave her the impression that he knew what it was, that he had discussed her with someone. *It has nothing to do with the fact that you're a woman*...almost as if he knew exactly what it had to do with.

It seemed as if Ian realized he'd said something, too, because he withdrew his hand and looked a little guilty.

"What do you know?" she asked him.

"Who, me?" He looked startled. He looked down at his plate and then at the window. "I don't know what you're talking about."

He was lying. Chelsea could plainly see it. "Yes you do!" she cried. "You know something! What is it, Ian? Has Jason said something about me?"

"No," he scoffed. But he stood up and picked up his plate. "I wish Brad had beer."

She jumped up to follow him. "Why won't you tell me? It can't be *that* bad."

"There's nothing to tell," Ian said.

"I don't believe you. Does it have to do with the Tesla account?"

She saw the hitch in his shoulders, but Ian put his plate in the sink, turned around to her, put his hands on her shoulders, and said, "I am telling you the truth. Jason has not said a word to me about you since I came here."

Chelsea studied his face a moment, looking for any sign of deception. He steadily held her gaze. "Okay," she said, nodding. She didn't believe him for a minute. She would get it out of him—she was tenacious that way.

Ian seemed to relax then and took her plate from her.

"I'll just ask Jason myself," she said, watching him.

"Good. Seems like the way to go." He began to run water, looking a little keyed up and studiously avoiding eye contact with her.

When they had finished cleaning up what little mess they'd made, Chelsea wandered out of the kitchen and stood at Brad's windows, looking out onto the sea of white.

Ian joined her, standing close and watching the snow fall. "What time is it?" he asked.

Chelsea glanced at her wristwatch. "Seven thirty." She peered up at him.

Ian looked at her. He slowly turned toward her,

and Chelsea shifted around a bit too. She felt a challenge in his gaze, but it was a different sort of challenge than what she had anticipated. They were standing quite close and Ian's glittering blue eyes were roaming around her face. His gaze slowly slid down to her mouth. She noticed his lips, too, full and soft and with the permanent hook of a near grin in one corner. In the low light of the generator and the utter quiet in the city, Chelsea could feel something arcing through her. A current of desire with a tail of pure lust.

For Ian Rafferty? Was she insane?

Ian's gaze went lower, to her chest, and he said, "It's going to be a long night. Wonder how we'll amuse ourselves."

"What is *that* supposed to mean?" she asked softly. Did it mean what she thought it meant? Or had she completely lost her mind and it was *she* who wanted it to mean something? Because no matter what she thought of Ian Rafferty when it came to her job, the man was sexy as hell.

"What do you think it means?"

She was losing it. She could really use a drink, and a thought occurred to her. "Have you ever talked about the Knicks in the partners' conference room?"

"Huh?" he muttered, and he brushed a bit of her hair from her shoulder.

"I know where they keep the booze."

Ian's gaze came up at that. "Serious?"

"As a sermon," she said. "We just need to find a key. But I think I know where one is."

Ian grinned, and the sight of it was electrifying. He yanked his tie free of his collar. "Let's *do* this," he said and he put an arm around her shoulder, leading her out of Brad's office.

Chapter 6

IAN HAD MET MR. GRABBER'S ASSISTANT, Andrea Slater, only once or twice. But he knew she was the grande dame of the assistants around here, having sat in this seat longer than anyone else at the company.

Ian and Zimmerman liked to joke about what Andrea did. As the senior partner, Grabber was rarely in the office, but Andrea was here every day. Ian had seen Andrea knitting, had seen her with a game of solitaire on her computer, and one day, when he'd seen her with her back to the door, he was convinced she'd been sleeping.

Chelsea walked around behind Andrea's desk as if it were familiar to her and opened a drawer, lifting up the files there to look underneath.

"What are you doing?" Ian asked uncomfortably.

"Looking for the key." She closed that drawer and opened another one and moved things around.

Even though there was no one in the office, Ian couldn't help looking anxiously over his shoulder, waiting for someone to catch them. "Do you really think you should be looking in her desk?"

Chelsea closed that drawer and opened a third.

"Chelsea—"

"Aha!" she cried, and she held up a ring of keys, making them jingle, her smile triumphant.

"Okay, let's go," he said, motioning for her to come around from behind Andrea's desk. He put a hand to the small of her back and hurried her along, forcing her to walk so quickly she had to take a couple of hops, getting them away from the scene of the crime as he scanned the fixtures for any sign of a hidden camera.

"Don't be so nervous," Chelsea said, reading him easily. "It's just a key."

"It's her *desk*."

"Right. And it was Paulson's fridge, but I didn't notice you worrying about that."

"How can you not see that surviving and snooping are entirely two different things?" he demanded.

"It's exactly the same thing!" she insisted as they reached the door of the conference room.

"Just open the door," he said impatiently.

Chelsea tried a key. It wouldn't turn. Ian would have gone onto the next key, but she withdrew it and tried it again, as if she thought she hadn't inserted it correctly. "Well, this one doesn't work."

Ian tried not to tap his foot as she tested the next one and, again, made several attempts when the key clearly would not turn.

"Here, let me," he said, reaching for the keys, but Chelsea slapped his hand away. "Stop it. I think I can open a door!"

"Do you think you can do it tonight?"

She stopped what she was doing to level the look of an irked female on him. "Okay, *you* need to calm down now. Slow and steady always wins the race."

"Not this one. You're too slow. No one has this kind of time."

"Are you kidding? We have nothing *but* time." She turned back to the door and tried another key.

Ian groaned and sank against the wall as she tried another one. And another.

She went through at least ten keys before she tossed her head back and sighed to the ceiling. "These aren't the right keys."

"Yes they are," he said and motioned for the keys. "Give 'em."

"Did you not just see me go through them all?"

"Yes. Every single one of them, turning them this way and that like a little kid. Some keys need to be jiggled and coaxed. Let me," Ian said, and he grabbed her wrist in one hand, lifted her arm, and pried the keys from her fingers with the other hand.

Chelsea bowed grandly and gestured to the door. "By all means, Mr. Rafferty. Show me your superior door-opening skills."

Ian began the process again while Chelsea stood by his side, her hands on her hips, muttering a variety of *I told you so's*. It wasn't long before he realized he was going to be forced to concede that these were not the right keys. He groaned. "You're right," he forced himself to say.

She smiled with far too much pleasure. "Of course I'm right. I won't say I told you so *again*, but we both know I did," she said smartly and took the keys from him. "This is the wrong set. Which makes no sense, seeing as how we are an office of doorless cubes. How many keys could this office possibly need?"

Ian didn't care. He only cared that a drink was not in his future. "I guess that's that."

"That's that? You give up too easily!"

"Do you have any bright ideas? Besides riffling through everyone's desk and personal things?"

Chelsea suddenly gasped, startling him. "I know who has them!" She grabbed his hand, pulling him along now. She dropped his hand in Andrea's office and darted around the desk to return the keys.

She opened the drawer she'd found them in. "Marian Zarin. Know her?"

"No."

"Short? Reddish hair?" Chelsea said as she returned the keys to the place where she'd found them. "She's different but…" Something caught her eye. She picked up a paper from the drawer.

"But what?" Ian asked.

"Different," she said absently, her gaze on the paper.

"You said that." He looked at the paper now too. "What do you have?"

Chelsea was not listening to him. She squinted at the paper and then suddenly gasped, her eyes going wide. "Oh my *God*," she said disbelievingly.

"Chelsea? What do you have?" He walked around the desk and looked over her shoulder and saw the title of the paper she held. It was a salary chart. "Hey, put that back," he said reaching for it.

But Chelsea was too fast for him. She jerked the paper out of his reach and lunged away from him.

"Put it *back*," he said more sternly. The last thing he needed was for her to see how much he made, especially now that they seemed to actually be making some progress with each other. But Chelsea ignored him, her gaze on the chart. "That is none of your business," he said. He couldn't imagine a worse breach than to see the private salary of everyone in this office.

"Aren't you the slightest bit curious?"

"Of course I'm curious." He'd say more than curious. "But you took that without permission from Andrea's drawer, which is so lacking in integrity that you ought to be fired."

"Please, like I don't know that," she said dismissively, as if knowing what she was doing was wrong somehow absolved her. "But it's not like I went looking for it, Ian. It just so happens this is what I found when I was looking for keys, which you have already said was a matter of survival."

"What? I never said—"

"*My* salary is on here, you know. So is Zimmerman's." She arched a brow, silently daring him to order her to put it back now.

And much to Ian's chagrin, he hesitated. He liked hanging out with Zimmerman, but he wasn't quite sure what he actually *did*. He never seemed to have any accounts to work on. And Ian was definitely curious what they were paying Chelsea.

"Probably yours too," she said slyly.

Ian made a sudden move and tried to snatch it out of her hand. Chelsea jerked it out of his reach again. That was the exact wrong thing to do.

Chelsea seemed to know it was, because she suddenly darted out of the office with the chart.

Ian was quickly behind her, hindered only by Andrea's desk. By the time he reached the door, Chelsea had disappeared into the sea of cubes.

"Do you really think this is going to work?" he called out, moving stealthily down the aisle and checking each cubicle. "What are we, seven years old? Just put the chart back, Chelsea."

She suddenly darted out of Jeff Bower's cubicle just in front of him. Ian dove for her, making contact with her arm. With a squeal, Chelsea managed to dance beyond his reach and then ran down the aisle.

She was fast, but she wasn't as fast as Ian. He caught up to her at the end of the aisle and launched himself at her, crashing with her into the glass wall of the conference room. But when Chelsea cried out as if he'd hurt her, he instantly let go. She jumped again, turned around, and laughed. "Ha!"

"You don't play fair," he said, and with his back to the glass wall, he slid down to the floor.

"Neither do you," Chelsea said and stood over him, her legs braced apart. "You want to see this chart? Tell me what Jason told you and I'll give it to you."

He couldn't believe either her incredible

perception or her lucky, but accurate, read of him. Not to mention her audacity for using a salary chart like this. He pretended to roll onto his hands and knees, but in the last moment, he grabbed her ankle. He didn't mean to topple her over, but down she went, landing on her bum. Ian scrambled, pinning her firmly on the floor, holding her arm and the paper she gripped above her head.

"You are…" Ian's voice trailed off. Her eyes were shining with ire, her chest rising and falling with each furious breath. She was close enough to kiss. This was twice in the space of about fifteen minutes, and in that moment, on a floor that smelled faintly of solvent, with her dark hair spilling around her, he wanted to kiss her. This was not a general, kiss-a-girl desire but a burning one. Red hot. Consuming.

"You *knocked* me *down*," she said, as if he was unaware of what he'd just done.

"You brought it on yourself," he said. His gaze slid to her mouth again.

"What are you looking at?" she demanded. She kicked him, managing to connect with his ankle.

"Ow, ow, ow," he said, grimacing.

"Let me up!"

Ian grabbed her hand, yanked the salary chart from it, and shifted off of her. He pulled her up, and as Chelsea rearranged her skirt, he looked at the paper. "Wait," he said, his brow knitting with confusion. "There are no salaries on here."

"Nope," she said as she pushed her hair from her face. "What kind of person do you take me for?"

A clever one. The chart was titled, and the employee names were listed in alphabetical order. Next to them were their cube numbers and phone numbers. But the column for the salary information had been left blank.

"I can't believe this," he said, holding the paper up. "I can't believe you just used this chart to *trick* me."

"Can't you?" Chelsea's hands found her waist. "Are you going to tell me now?" she asked, poking him.

"I've told you. I don't know anything."

"Liar." Chelsea cocked her head to one side and brushed something from his cheek. "Not a very good one, either. I would have thought you'd be really good at it. How about that drink?"

"*Yes*," he said.

She smiled. "Follow me."

She led him through the cubes to one that had a sign hanging on the outside that said, *Think Tank: Shark-Infested Waters.*

"You'd have to know Marian," Chelsea said.

"She comes off as really strange. But she's brilliant with advertising." She disappeared inside, and Ian followed her, hesitating only once when he saw the mess in Marian's cube. It made his cube look neat and organized. The level of chaos was ridiculous— papers were stacked high on the desk, with only a small space cleared for working. There were used plates and cups, dusty holiday tinsel, and sacks marked with the H&M logo from which protruded clothes with tags on them. There were Post-its with a scrawling handwriting on them, pictures of people, lots of people, and a calendar that was two years old. There were three potted plants on the floor—all dead—and a pile of shoes that looked as if someone had been gathering them up to give to charity.

But on the wall behind the desk were several framed commendations and employee awards.

"*This* person has keys? Because the last thing this person needs are keys to the liquor cabinet."

Chelsea laughed. "I can't disagree." She stepped gingerly over the trash on the floor, leaning over the bags so far that her most excellent derriere was presented to him. She reached the keys and then popped up and around, holding another set of keys. "Here they are!" she said brightly. And then she frowned, having caught Ian in the act of admiring her bottom.

He smiled guiltily and nervously dragged his fingers through his hair.

"Really?" Chelsea said impatiently.

"Hey," he said, throwing his hands up. "I can't help but admire an excellent figure. I won't say more than that because I don't want anyone in this cubicle to call me a lech," he said, pointing at her.

"Wise move." She walked past him, carelessly bumping into him as she hopped over some things on the floor.

Chelsea did possess a very nice ass, Ian thought as he followed her back to the conference room. One he would like to put his hands on.

Ian watched as she opened the door to the conference room. "Ta-da!" she said, and she jingled the keys at him before sticking them back in the door. She went in ahead of him, crossed the room, and threw open floor-to-ceiling cabinet doors. At least Ian had assumed they were cabinet doors all this time. They actually opened to reveal a full bar, complete with a sink. There were glasses of various sizes, and there, on a glass shelf, was an assortment of liquor. Good liquor too.

Chelsea walked around behind the bar. "They use this room for client appreciation days and Christmas parties. I guess we haven't had one since you've been here. So what's your pleasure, vodka, tequila, or gin?"

"All of the above. Is there any tonic?" he asked.

Chelsea stooped down behind the cabinetry and then stood back up and held out a bottle of tonic water.

"Excellent. Give me the tonic and the vodka, and I'll make you a drink. I used to be a bartender."

"When?" she asked, handing him the vodka and tonic as he came behind the bar.

"College. It paid the bills."

"So *that's* where you got the skills for the wad of cash they are paying you," she said, and she dipped down again, reemerging with two highball glasses.

Ian slanted her a look as he poured some vodka into two glasses. "How long are you going to be mad about that?"

"For a while," she said with an easy smile.

She was a funny woman. "Chelsea, look—"

"Ah!" she said, instantly putting up her hand. "I would strongly advise that you not feed me some meaningless platitudes," she quickly interjected. "It's not right or fair, and you know it."

He really couldn't play devil's advocate on this one. She was right; it wasn't fair. If they weren't paying her as much as him, that was bad enough.

But they were going to have her pitch on an account she'd worked hard to get, even after deciding who they'd give the account to. It wasn't right, and it made him angry and uncomfortable. Frankly, he didn't get it—Chelsea was smart and clever and she did good work.

"What?" she said.

Ian realized he'd stopped mixing the drinks.

"I was just thinking…I hope you don't hate me for it, because I like you, Chelsea. And you're right, it's not fair."

She smiled with surprise. "Wow. *Thank* you, Ian. And for what it's worth, I don't hate you." She paused as if rethinking that and then shrugged a little. "Okay, maybe I hated you a bit when you started getting the accounts that should have been mine," she said, holding up a thumb and finger to show him just how little. "But really? I hate Jason. I hate him passionately right now." She took a bigger sip of her drink. "If he were here right now, I'd have to kill him, and it would be very messy. A lot of stomping and kicking." With her glass in hand, she began to walk around the conference room. "But you know what I *really* hate?" she said over her shoulder. "That it's my own fault. That's what makes me so mad, you know? I have let Jason use me and I know it. I've let him take my best ideas without thinking twice about what they were worth."

That, Ian knew, was a hard lesson to learn. Creative thinking was so hard to assign a value to, and yet it was one of the hardest jobs there was. Chelsea wasn't the first person to have misjudged the value of her ideas. Ian could guess that there had been times she should have asked for raises and didn't. Times she should have made Jason spell out her worth to this company and didn't do that, either.

He was starting to feel sick about how she would take the news when she found out that they had given him the Tesla account, and he downed his drink to push that away.

"You know my problem?" she asked rhetorically. "I am too trusting of men. It affects all my relationships." She laughed at that. "But you know how men are," she added with a sigh.

"Careful," Ian said. "No broad swipes at the entire male race, Crawford."

"Don't take it personally," she said cheerfully.

"How does your boyfriend take it?" he asked, suddenly very curious if she had one. He was even a bit surprised by how much he was hoping she did not.

"*Anh*," she said with a flick of her wrist. "We've kind of called it off. Wasn't working out."

"Oh yeah?" he asked, very curious now. "What's his name?"

"Brody."

Ian scowled. "Sounds like an actor."

Chelsea grinned. "Worse—he's a senator's aide."

"Wow," Ian said. "My sincerest condolences."

Chelsea laughed, unoffended. He realized that was something else about her he really liked—she was not easily offended.

"Well, that's why we're off. He's in DC all the time, and he says I work too many hours. He wants me to drop everything when he comes up from Washington, which, you know, he hasn't done in a while. I think because the last time he was here, I told him that he seemed to think his job was more important than mine. Apparently, I was right." She winked at Ian as she sipped from her glass. "You make a great vodka martini, by the way."

"It's a vodka tonic," he said.

"Whatever. I'm not really much of a drinker. I don't really even know if it's good or not. Okay, your turn, Rafferty. Girlfriend?"

Ian considered how best to answer that question. He didn't think the truth was going to do him any favors, the truth being that he was basically a dog, preferring to play the field rather than settle down with one woman. And then again, what difference did it make? It wasn't like he was trying to impress Chelsea. Was it?

"I am between girlfriends," he said, making quote marks with his fingers.

"Interesting. I think Nadia thinks it is more than that."

He'd forgotten about Nadia, a short, curly-blond-haired woman who worked in production. He'd run into her twice outside of work, and both times they had "hung out" in a very adult and ill-advised way at her apartment. "You're keeping up with me. I'm flattered," he said.

"I can't help but keep up with you. People talk. A *lot*. Especially about you."

"Why?" he asked curiously.

"*Why?* Because you're good at your job, and you're a flirt, and you're super cute."

He was surprisingly flattered that she'd said he was cute.

Chelsea sat on the conference table and leaned across it, sliding her glass to him. "But a friendly word of advice? Steer clear of Nadia. The last guy she dated broke it off and she started following him around town."

That startled Ian; Chelsea laughed at his expression, clearly enjoying the strike of fear.

"Thanks for the warning," he said. He picked up her glass and started back to the bar. "I don't have anything going on with Nadia, by the way. Never did. I hung out with her a couple of times, but I can spot crazy a mile away. We had a mutual understanding that it was just a friendly sort of thing."

"Famous last words," Chelsea said. "Funny thing about those mutual understandings," she continued as Ian poured them another round. "They're rarely truly mutual. Like this thing with Tesla. I thought Jason and I had a mutual understanding."

Ian was sure that was true. Jason was pretty good about making things sound definite when they weren't. He brought the drinks out and sat on the conference table next to Chelsea. When she took the glass from him, her fingers grazed his, and he felt a dozen little sparks fire in his skin. Which, for some inexplicable reason, made him think of how her mouth would taste.

Ian shifted his attention to the window and away from temptation.

A long moment passed in which they remained sitting next to each other, staring out at a silent snowy night, each with their own thoughts. Ian was thinking about Chelsea and how she had surprised him tonight. She wasn't as uptight as he'd believed her to be. She was actually a lot of fun. He could honestly say that if he was ever stuck in a snow-storm, he would like to have her along. Actually, he wouldn't mind having her along on other adventures. *Whoa*…was he really thinking that?

But he looked at Chelsea now, and he could picture it. The two of them, on a beach, in the mountains, sitting at a little table for two in a diner and arguing about the Knicks or the meaning of the movie they'd just seen. Strolling arm in arm around Central Park.

Chelsea, however, was apparently thinking of tomorrow, because she said wistfully, "My new office is going to have this same view."

That effectively ruined the pleasant vignettes, because Chelsea would probably never speak to him again after tomorrow.

Chelsea playfully nudged him with her shoulder when he didn't respond. "The office goes with the Tesla account. Didn't Jason tell you?"

"Yes, he told me." He hid the twinge of guilt he felt beneath a sip of his drink.

"Hey…" Chelsea put her glass aside. "Listen, I feel like I should tell you something while we're here, and, you know, being friends."

"Tell me what?"

"Just that Jason told me up front this was my account to lose. I mean, yes, he's a douchebag for the most part. But I don't think he'd lie about this." She nervously chewed her bottom lip. "Do you?"

Ian could feel the guilt, the regret, all of it, sliding over him like a blanket, weighing him down. He hadn't even done anything but take a phone call, and yet, he felt as if what he was doing right now was technically lying to her. He debated what he should do in this moment, and in his hesitation, she leaned forward to peer at him. "There it is again. That look—like you're a big fat cat who just ate the canary. Come on, Ian. I know Jason told you something. Did he tell you the same thing? Because that would not surprise me."

"No," he said quickly, and as Chelsea's gaze narrowed suspiciously, he said, "I promise you, Jason Sung has not said anything to me about you. Nor did he tell me this was my account to lose."

"Hmm," she said skeptically.

Damn it, this woman had a way of looking at him that made him feel as if she could see every thought in his head. "Why Tesla, Chelsea?" he blurted. "I mean, do you like cars?"

"What a weird question, coming from an ad man," she said with a wry smile. "Do I have to like cars? Tesla is a huge account. It's the natural progression of my work."

"Car accounts are the natural progression of your portfolio?"

"Big accounts are the natural progression of my portfolio."

"But I mean, do you *like* cars?"

Chelsea laughed. "I don't know. I've never owned one."

Ian put his drink aside. He had the crazy thought that if he made her see she didn't care that much about cars anyway, somehow she'd be all right when the truth came down. He realized he was grasping at ideas, but it was the only one he had. He didn't want to ruin this thing between them. He'd told Brad he wouldn't say a word. What was he supposed to do? He needed more than a few moments to think it through and decide. So he kept babbling. "So why not a big food account? Or pharmaceuticals? Or insurance?"

Chelsea looked at him as if he were talking gibberish. "Why not cars?" She smiled and swayed into him a little, almost as if the force of her smile had made her teeter off balance. "I believe in my abilities, in what it takes to reach an American audience. The product doesn't matter, because I will learn it and I will figure out what consumers want from it."

Ian nodded and polished off his drink. He

knew what she was saying; he felt the same way. That's what made him good at advertising, and it was the same thing that made her good. Which meant there was no way to soften the blow of what was coming.

"What's the matter now, Rafferty?" she teased him. "You're not worried about the competition, are you?"

He smiled and tucked an errant strand of hair behind her ear.

She held out her hand to him. "Okay, I won't tease you. May the best man win."

Ian looked at her hand. He wove his fingers in through hers. He felt like a jerk. He wished there wasn't a Tesla account. He wished Grabber-Paulson had never come to him, because he did not want to be the guy who was going to crush her.

Chelsea squeezed his fingers lightly. "You're still holding my hand."

"I am, aren't I?" he said absently.

"So…what are we doing?" Chelsea asked, her voice softer.

"I don't know," Ian admitted. He didn't know anything other than he was feeling a strangely intoxicating mix of guilt and desire and affection. He felt off center, out of control.

"I'm not an office hookup, you know," she said, her fingers still curling around his.

He arched a brow at her. "Did I make a pass?"

"No." She smiled sheepishly. "You know, I'm starting to wonder if maybe I misjudged you."

That brought a rush of heat to his neck. He touched her hair, feeling the heft of it between his finger and thumb. "How so?"

Her gaze settled on his mouth. "All this time I thought you were an arrogant player, with no redeeming qualities."

"Guilty," he said with a grin, and he shifted closer, touching his nose to her hair. "And now?"

"Now, I think there is more to you than that. You're a nice guy, Ian. And you're..."

"Talented? Brilliant?"

She laughed softly. "Cute."

"Ah," he said and nibbled her earlobe. "I'm also a sucker for an attractive woman."

She sighed and angled her head a little as he moved down to nuzzle her neck. "I bet you've said that five times this week alone."

"Not true," he said and kissed her neck. He liked the way she tasted. He liked the way she smelled. "I don't generally have to say anything."

Chelsea's head came around at that, and Ian laughed. "Kidding."

She touched her finger to his lips. "Are we flirting?" she asked.

"Are we?"

"I think so. In the interest of fair play, I think you should know that I will take any advantage of anything I can tomorrow. I really, really hate to lose."

"I've noticed. You must believe I have a soft spot to tell me that," Ian said, and he touched his lips to hers. "But I don't. I hate losing too. But I've been strangely attracted to you since the moment I met you. I took one look in your cubicle, with all the papers stacked just so and the pictures of your family tacked to the walls, and I thought, here is a woman who cares about what she's doing. I can get into that." He kissed her again, light and easy, a prelude to what he really wanted, to the craving beating in his chest and pounding in his veins.

"You looked at my cube?" she asked with a smile of delight.

"I looked at your cube, I looked at your body, and I looked at your hair…" He pushed her hair back and nibbled her earlobe. "I even smelled you."

"*Weird*," she said. But she did not sound put off by it.

Ian found her waist with his hand and began to slowly slide it up her rib cage. "And you know those shoes you were wearing in the conference room today? I *definitely* noticed your legs in those shoes."

"I am so onto you, Ian," she said, and she touched two fingers to his mouth. "You must believe that *I* have a soft spot. I don't."

"Then I guess that makes us perfect for each other, doesn't it?" he said as his hand slid up and cupped her breast. "Maybe, on this little snow island of ours, we can put aside our jobs and our competition and just, you know…enjoy the moment."

She drew a slow, unsteady breath. "You really think that's a good idea?"

He thought it was perhaps the best idea he'd ever had. He'd thought his brilliance was in advertising, but *this* was his brilliance. He was melting inside, his body responding to the feel of her, to her scent, her sparkly green eyes, and her smile. "I think we'd be idiots if we didn't," he said, and he meant it sincerely. He couldn't remember feeling this sort of sizzle in a very long time. He caught her chin in his hand, turned her face to his, and kissed her. He kissed her fully this time, and it sent a shock wave through him, pouring through every vein, every muscle.

Chelsea grabbed the collar of his shirt and held on, responding in kind, flicking her tongue against his.

If he'd known Chelsea Crawford could kiss like this, he wouldn't have screwed around—it was electric, pulse pounding. Ian was suddenly working on overdrive, an engine revved up too fast. He slid off the conference table, put his arm around her, and pulled her to him, sliding in between her legs. His body had sprung to attention, ready and waiting for whatever Chelsea would allow.

Ian was hopeful on that front, as Chelsea made a sound in the back of her throat that sounded very much like desire to him. All the male in him was rejoicing in the teamwork here, how two people could come together and make something *utterly fantastic* happen, without any pretense of dates and late-night phone calls. It was meant to be, as if they'd been caught in this storm for this reason, and Ian thought he'd never been so excited in his whole freaking life. He completely forgot that he expressly didn't *want* to do this, that he felt guilty and sort of gross knowing what he knew, and that he never liked to get involved, especially at work.

He forgot all that because Chelsea felt and tasted so damn good, and she was different in that she didn't really even like him. That made her special, that made her incredibly desirable, and this was going to be one of the best nights of his life—

Until Chelsea suddenly slid off the table and out from underneath his touch.

"No, no, no," he said, sensing doom, and he tried to draw her back. But Chelsea moved beyond his reach. "Come on, Chelsea," he said, aware that he sounded a little whiny. "Don't go. If you don't want to do this," he said, forcing himself to say those words, because how could she *not*, "that's cool. But don't be offended. Don't go. Let's just… let's just have another drink and watch the snow."

"I'm not offended," she said. "But I'm not an idiot, either."

"Don't say that," he said with a wince.

She flounced around and started for the door.

"Come on. Where are you going?" he called after her.

"For a walk!" she said, and she went right out of the conference room.

Ian groaned with physical frustration and slammed his fist down on the conference table. He instantly grimaced at the pain that caused him, stretching his fingers wide, fearing he'd broken a bone.

Chapter 7

CHELSEA SLIPPED INTO THE WOMEN'S BATHROOM and gripped the counter edge, drawing deep, steadying breaths. She wasn't really thinking what she was thinking, was she? She wasn't seriously considering having sex with Ian Rafferty in the conference room…*was she*?

"*Ohmigod*, I am," she said under her breath to her reflection in the milky bathroom light. "You have totally lost your mind." She used her fingers to try to repair hair that looked wild after a day of wind and snow and running around with salary charts. Her mascara had smudged under her eyes, which she quickly swiped clean with a tissue.

She was not going back in there. She wasn't. It was ridiculous! Not only was it inappropriate as hell, she should be using this time to go over her pitch, to review her ad. And besides, she was not the sort of person to have a one-night fling.

She was a three-date girl—at least three real dates before she would even consider it. She was definitely *not* the type to have a one-time fling with an office mate who, until a few hours ago, she hadn't even liked.

But to hell with all that, argued the devil that had overtaken her body and was trying to snuff out her thoughts. Ian Rafferty was a very handsome man. And she liked him. Against all odds, she really liked him. It was shocking to her, but there it was—she was very attracted to a handsome, *likable* man. What was the world coming to?

"But it's such a bad idea, Chelsea," she whined to her reflection again. "A really, seriously, stupendously bad idea. You know how it goes when these things happen in the office. Awkward meetings in the break room, gossip, sitting outside to eat your lunch day after day in the hope that you might see him? Because you know you will. You know how you are. You'll act like it's not a big deal when it is a very big deal to you. So yeah, no, Chelsea. Just *no*." She shook her head at herself and walked out of the women's bathroom.

And she kept walking, right around to the office foyer, where her things were still lying on the floor where she'd left them. The candy bars, her tote bag, her Very Expensive Shoes. Chelsea leaned down, untied the laces of her tennis shoes, and kicked them off. She took her new shoes from their protective sleeves and put them on.

"Who *are* you?" she muttered and began striding for the conference room. "When did you become this woman? When did you throw all your principles out the window for sex? Yes, okay, it has all the markings of being *fabulous* sex, but still."

She reached the doors, took a breath, and put her hand on the handle. "You know what you are?" she said, and she yanked the door open, startling Ian as she walked in. He was still on the conference table, the highball glass dangling between his fingers. He'd pulled his shirttail free of his trousers and had undone a couple of buttons. He eyed her apprehensively, as if he expected her to come in and do something to his person.

But then his gaze moved down her body, to her legs, braced apart, and her shoes.

"I am an idiot," she said, answering her question to herself.

Ian's eyes sparked. He slowly slid off the conference table, his gaze raking over her, taking in every inch of her. "Then that makes two of us. Like I said, perfect for each other." He put down the glass.

There was no going back, Chelsea realized.

Ian was moving toward her, his gaze wolfish. "Nice shoes," he said, his voice low. "Don't take them off." He reached for her—with eagerness, with desire—and Chelsea could feel something electric slipping through her. Excitement, relief, decadence—all the things that made every inch of her body sizzle with anticipation.

When he slid his hand under her blouse and up to her breast, her body took over all her thinking, and the next thing she knew, her blouse was open, his mouth was on her breast.

They performed an erotic dance around that conference room—Ian twirling her around, pushing her up against a column, and pressing his erection into her hips. Chelsea pushing him into a chair so that she could free his cock. Ian grabbing her by the hips and lifting her up to the conference table, caressing her legs as he moved in between them. Chelsea arching her back, pressing her tongue into his mouth, her hands in his hair, her breasts against his chest. And there were sounds coming from her, sounds of pure pleasure that she didn't think she made often. She was hot and wet, eager to go wherever he would take her.

Somehow, Chelsea's bra came off. Somehow, his shirt was gone, too, revealing a muscular chest and arms. His hands were wild on her body, caressing her breasts, pinching her nipples, sliding in between her legs and into her body. Chelsea's breath was deliciously short; she caught his head, kissed him deeply, biting lightly against his bottom lip as he melted onto the floor with her. She moved her hands down his body, over his chest, down his sides to his hips, and took him in hand, stroking him.

Ian groaned. His fingers sank deep in the soft folds of her flesh as he sank his body into hers, sliding deep. Chelsea wrapped her legs around his waist, her shoes dangling above his back. He filled his mouth with her breast and began to move. Slow and steady, tantalizing and deep.

"*Oh God*," she whispered as he moved so expertly inside her, his hand on her sex, moving with his body. It felt as if she'd never done this before, and maybe she hadn't, not like this. The feel of his body next to hers was more arousing than that of any man she'd ever been with. She opened her eyes and saw that he was watching her, his blue eyes gone dark. That look—one of utter desire—lit something deep inside Chelsea, in a place where nothing else mattered than this sort of connection with another person. It was moving, it was touching—it was so many things that she didn't want it to be and, yet, would be devastated to have missed.

He began to quicken the pace, and Chelsea began to move with him, meeting his rhythm, desperate for the release that was building. When she came, Ian followed her with a groan of ecstasy.

He sagged against her. After a moment, he pushed her hair from her neck and face and tenderly kissed her. "You amaze me," he said, and he propped himself up to stroke her cheek.

His gaze roamed her face as he traced a line across her chin. "That was…something else."

"Yeah," Chelsea agreed, and she brushed his hair from his forehead.

He continued to take her in, his hand following his eyes, brushing against her breasts, caressing her abdomen, and kissing the inside of her leg.

Chelsea turned her head and happened to notice her bra on the back of a chair. Various pieces of clothing were scattered around the conference room. Chelsea couldn't help giggling.

Ian chuckled too and kissed her again.

There were so many conflicting thoughts running around Chelsea's head. She really liked him, and she wanted to say so. But there was the Tesla account and the tiny little voice in the back of her head that reminded her that Ian had warned he was the kind to play the field, that this had been a one-night stand for him.

"What are you thinking?" Ian asked her.

"That you're a surprising guy. And that I can't believe that just happened."

"It happened. And it was spectacular."

"Yeah," she said, smiling happily. "The only thing that could make it perfect would be food. I'm hungry."

He laughed. "Lean Cuisine?"

"Great sex and Lean Cuisine. It's perfect."

They picked themselves up off the floor and began to gather their clothing. But as Ian handed Chelsea her bra, he said, "This really is perfect, Chelsea." He gestured to the two of them and the room, the windows. "We should have thought of this a long time ago."

Chelsea laughed. If one was going to get stuck in a blizzard, this was the way to go, hands down.

—◆◆◆—

In Brad's office, which was beginning to feel as familiar to Chelsea as her own cubicle, they dined on more Lean Cuisine—agreeing to leave two in the freezer so that Brad wouldn't be completely pissed—and a jar of pickles she'd found in the break room.

They talked like old friends.

Ian asked about her desire to write, and Chelsea admitted to Ian that she had a book she'd been working on for several months. She was always a little reticent to say that out loud, and in fact, the only other person she'd told was Brody, who had advised her to focus on advertising. Ian was interested in the book and what her plan was once she'd finished it. "I know an editor at Random House," he said.

"You do?" she asked, surprised and elated by this.

"Dated her," he said. "I'd be happy to ask her if she'd take a look if you want."

"Well…how did it end between you two?"

He laughed. "We're good. It was mutual."

"Then I accept your offer. That would be fantastic!" Chelsea said. "Thank you! What about you? Have you written anything?"

"Nah," he said with a charming grin. "I think about it, but I'm not as disciplined as you. Most days, it's all I can do to work here."

They talked about the accounts they'd had too—the lessons learned, the worst and best accounts in their career thus far. Ian was most proud of his work on the luxury vehicle brand Infiniti. He was proud of the increase in sales after he'd taken over the campaign. Chelsea's best account was a small regional cupcake chain. "I love the idea I came up with—a premenstrual woman on the hunt for a cupcake fix but one that wouldn't add to her water weight woes. And the benefits of having that account were excellent—some of the best cupcakes I've ever had in my life. Plus, they were able to open up three new stores after those ads ran."

"That reminds me of—" Ian started, but then the lights suddenly flicked on. They both gasped with surprise as they looked around at the flood of light. And then they looked at each other. Ian was clearly thinking the same thing as Chelsea, because he jumped up at the same time she did. "I'll get this—you get the conference room!"

She didn't have to ask him what he meant— they both moved as if they expected a SWAT team to burst in and discover they'd made themselves at home in the corporate offices amid empty Lean Cuisine trays and vodka bottles.

When Ian joined Chelsea in the conference room, Chelsea couldn't help but laugh. "I think we're safe."

Ian helped her close the big cabinet doors. She fastened the little latch and turned around, her back to the door. Ian was still standing there, an affectionate smile on his face. "So what do you think, Crawford? Are things going to change between us?"

"Are you referring to our rivalry?"

Ian took her elbow in hand and pulled her close, wrapping his arms around her. "Are we rivals?"

"Of course," she said, pausing to allow him to kiss her. "Have to be. It keeps us on our creative toes."

"I like this version of us better," he said, and he kissed her again.

"Me too."

He paused in his languid kissing of her and stared down at her as if he were trying to discern something. "We could see where this goes."

Chelsea smiled. "Are you serious?"

"Yes."

She straightened his collar and shook her head. "It would never work, Ian. It would be weird. Think about it—depending on who gets the account tomorrow, it could be really awkward."

"Wow," he said, and he looked, remarkably, a little hurt.

"I'm sorry," she said with a wince. "I'm just being practical."

"Practical? There wasn't one thing that happened tonight that was practical, and I, for one, really liked it. I don't know how it would work, but I don't want to throw away what happened here between us."

He had a point. "Okay," she said. "Can we let it stew a little?" She twirled a bit of his hair around her finger. "I mean, tomorrow, we might feel differently."

"Yeah," Ian said, and his arms slid away from her. "About tomorrow…"

Chelsea's stomach immediately began to sink. "What about it?"

He sighed uneasily, and her gut sank lower.

"You were right. I do know something."

Chelsea's breath caught. And then she punched him in the chest. "I *knew* it!" she cried. "Why didn't you tell me? What is it? What did that dirtbag Jason tell you?"

"Not Jason," he said, shaking his head. "That's true—Jason hasn't said anything to me." He shoved his hands in his pockets, and, for the first time since Chelsea had met him, he looked uncomfortable in his skin.

"Okay, then who?" she pressed.

"Brad," he said.

Chelsea felt sick.

"He called me yesterday. He told me the partners had made up their minds and they are giving Tesla to me."

That was impossible. It made no sense! Chelsea

looked wildly about the room. "But we haven't even *pitched*—"

"I know, I know," he said. "That's the part that sucks the most. They are going to have us present our ads…but they've decided."

There were no words to describe her emotions. Chelsea felt betrayed, emotionally shattered, and nauseous with disbelief at the shamelessness of it.

"Chelsea," Ian said quietly, and he reached for her, but Chelsea batted his hand away.

"How could they?" she asked, folding her arms tightly around her, feeling cold. "My work on this account is *good*." She began to pace, trying to work it out in her head, where it had gone wrong. "Safety and innovation come together in this car," she said to Ian, reciting part of her pitch. She'd been over this. Her pitch was good, the ad was good, it was all so *good*. "It's a marriage of lifestyle to vehicle."

She had pictured the partners as she spoke, had imagined them looking at each other with expressions that said, *how did we miss this*?

"Tesla. Because you expect it." She looked at Ian. "That's my tagline! And it's a *great* tagline! They haven't heard it yet, so how do they know?" she cried, casting her arms wide.

"You're right. It's good. It's really good," he agreed.

"Then what the hell?" she asked plaintively. "What's wrong with my idea, Ian?"

Ian winced a little, and Chelsea felt a wave of disappointment. She hadn't realized until now how much she wanted Ian to like her work.

"Look, I haven't seen your ad. But I know that Jason and Brad think it might be a tad too…" He paused, as if trying to think of the right words.

"Don't tell me. Chrysler LeBaron Syndrome?"

"They never said that. That was me," he said. "But yeah. Something like that."

Chelsea blinked. And then she whirled around, her mind racing alongside her heart. Was he *right*? Had she geared her ad to an audience that was too old? Had she focused too much on the wealthy baby boomers?

She felt Ian behind her before he put his hand on her shoulder. She couldn't speak—she was too enraged, too hurt, too betrayed to speak. She wanted to push him away, but at the same time, as he slowly and carefully slipped his arm around her middle and pulled her into his chest, she needed his support.

She had worked so damn hard for Grabber-Paulson. She had been promised that her time was coming, and now that it was here, they were going to pass her over *again*. "I'm confused and mad and…and *crushed*," she admitted.

Ian didn't say anything. He rested his chin on the top of her head.

"I feel so *used*."

"What are you going to do?" he asked.

"I honestly don't know," she said.

"Chelsea, look, I—"

The front door alarm sounded, and Chelsea jumped. Ian quickly ushered her around to his back.

"I'll go look," he said, but before he could get very far, a security guard appeared in the hallway. He saw Chelsea and Ian through the windows and gave them a wave.

The security guard walked into the conference room and looked around. "How you folks doing tonight?"

"Who are you?" Ian asked.

"Night security," the man said. "Walking the floors to see if anyone was stranded by the power outage. Found four down on the twenty-first floor. Everyone in here okay?" he asked, leaning a little to his right to see Chelsea.

"We're fine," Ian said. "What's going on out there?"

"The elevators are working again," the security guy said. He hitched up his pants and looked around the room. "A couple of the subway lines are up and running too."

"You mean we can get out of here?" Chelsea asked, popping out from behind Ian. She needed to be as far from Grabber-Paulson as she could get. She needed some time to think and digest, to prepare for whatever it was she would do tomorrow.

"Depending on where you're going—"

"Brooklyn," Chelsea said.

"I think you can get there," the security guard said. "Anyone else in the office with you?"

"Just us," Ian confirmed.

"Well then, I'm going to go on and see if there is anyone else stuck inside."

"Thank you," Ian said. He watched the guard walk away and looked at Chelsea.

She thought that he wanted to say something, but Chelsea didn't want to talk. It had been a fantastic night with Ian, but now it was ruined. She was looking at the face of the man who would be sitting in her office, managing her account. She didn't blame Ian. But it wasn't okay.

"I'm getting out of here," she said, and she hurried past him to gather her things before he could stop her.

Chapter 8

CHELSEA DIDN'T SAY MUCH AS THEY MADE THEIR way to the subway, but then again, the wind was blowing and they were trudging through big drifts of snow.

Ian walked down into the subway with her. She stopped outside the turnstiles. "I'm going to Brooklyn. Where are you going?"

"Uptown," Ian said. His station was another two blocks up.

"Okay, well…" She brushed snow from her hat. "I guess this is where we part for now." She tried to smile, but Ian could see how wounded she felt.

"Chelsea, I'm sorry," he said. And he was, profoundly sorry. He could kick himself for it. "Should I have told you?"

She sighed. "Yes, you should have told me." She smiled at him then, and she touched her mitten to his hand. He hated to see the disappointment brimming in her eyes. It made him feel helpless. It also made him angry on her behalf.

"It's bad for me but great for you. Congratulations, Ian. It's not that I can't accept defeat. I just…really do not like my employer right now."

"Sure," he said, because he didn't know what else to say. He only knew he'd spent an incredible night with this woman, and he had felt things he'd not felt in a long time. Exuberance. Passion. Hope for nebulous things he really hadn't known he hoped for until tonight. And that had all been ruined by the games Grabber-Paulson had played with her.

"So…I'm going to go now," she said, pointing to her station. "I'm going to go and process this. But I'll see you tomorrow."

"Right," he said. She turned to go, but Ian caught her mittened hand and pulled her back. He wrapped her in an embrace and said, "Whatever happens, I just want you to know that tonight was…it was incredible," he said. "I know that's a weird thing to say, but I really…I hope things are okay between us."

He lowered his head to kiss her, but she suddenly rose up and kissed him on the corner of his mouth and then patted him on the chest. "Not to worry," she said lightly. "I'd better go." She turned and disappeared into the entrance to the subway.

Ian watched her walk down the steps until she had disappeared into the bowels of the subway.

And still, Ian didn't move. *That* was the worst brush-off kiss he'd ever received in his life. Hell, it may have been the *only* brush-off kiss he'd ever received. But that's what it was and Ian didn't like it, not one bit.

It took Ian two hours to get home. He showered and collapsed, exhausted, onto his bed.

A few hours later, he received a robo-call from Grabber-Paulson. It was Brad's cheerful voice informing employees that work was canceled due to the unusual spring blizzard. They would resume normal activities on Monday.

That gave Ian three full days to ruminate about Chelsea Crawford.

He wanted to talk to her, to explain that the night in the office had meant something to him. He wanted her to understand it was a big deal to him, because those sorts of encounters rarely meant so much to him. He didn't know exactly what it meant, but he knew he wasn't going to let it go without fighting for it.

Unfortunately, he didn't know how to get hold of Chelsea. By Saturday evening, he wanted to speak to her so badly that he swallowed his pride and called Zimmerman to ask if he had her number.

"Chelsea Crawford?" Zimmerman said. "Why?"

"Ah…to tell her the pitch is rescheduled."

"Why are *you* calling her to tell her? Why isn't Jason?"

Since when had Zimmerman been such a busybody? "Don't know. They asked me to do it."

"That seems weird, man," Zimmerman said.

"Do you have her number or not?" Ian demanded.

"No," Zimmerman said cheerfully. "Tell Jason or whoever put you up to it that admin is not your job."

"Yeah, okay. Thanks," Ian said. He got off the phone before Zimmerman could launch into chatting about himself, as he was wont to do.

Ian was cross and antsy, and his mood did not improve. He began to wonder if he'd just imagined the things he'd felt with Chelsea or if they were real. There was only one way to find out, but the city was only slowly crawling out from under the blizzard.

By Sunday, Ian felt he'd explode if he didn't get out of his apartment. He walked down the street to the gym and ran five miles on the treadmill.

That wasn't enough.

He ran two more, and still he felt mixed up, turned inside out, upside down, by a girl.

He ran ten miles, thinking about that night in the offices. Yes, he thought about the sex, but mostly he thought about Chelsea, and the way her eyes shimmered when she laughed, and how easy she was to get along with. *Easy!* And for these last few months, he'd thought her uptight and inflexible. But she wasn't like that at all, she was funny and warm and pretty and smart. She was all the things he liked in a woman.

He thought a lot about how this thing with Tesla had gone down. It was a horrible way to treat a trusted, productive employee, and Ian felt for Chelsea. He pictured her in an apartment in Brooklyn, staring at the television or maybe maniacally cleaning the toilet—

Okay, so he didn't know Chelsea well enough to know what she'd do in a situation like this. But he wanted to know. More than anything, he wanted to know.

Monday morning, the city had slid back into its usual grind. Ian dressed in his best blue suit. He thought a lot about the pitch, but before he left, he stared at himself a long time in the mirror.

The thrill of the pitch was missing, the hum of anticipation in his body absent. This was the thing he loved about his job. He loved going in, laying out an idea, watching the faces change from skepticism to excitement. He'd worked hard on Tesla, but this pitch felt different. It felt ugly and meaningless.

When he reached the office, it looked just as it had Thursday morning before the blizzard, and it was hard to believe he and Chelsea had spent that evening here. He walked past her cubicle and saw her tote bag on the desk. Her lights were on. She was here, somewhere in these walls, preparing to pitch as if she didn't know the truth.

Jason saw Ian, and still seated in his chair, he rolled into the opening of his office and said, "Dude! Looking sharp! You ready to do this thing? Ready to get a big account?" He waggled his brows.

"When are we doing it?" Ian asked.

"This morning," Jason said happily. "Get some coffee, clear out the cobwebs, and come to the partners' conference room at eleven."

Yeah, it would have to be the partners' conference room, wouldn't it?

Ian went through the motions of getting his act together. He accepted the good luck wishes of people walking by. He gave his ad to the tech guy to cue up. He swore to Zimmerman he wasn't nervous, and he wasn't. He just wanted it over.

At ten to eleven, he picked up his file with his notes, shoved one hand in his pocket, and walked around to the conference room. That was when he saw Chelsea for the first time since Thursday night.

She looked beautiful. Gorgeous. Had she always been this pretty? She was wearing her dark hair in a sleek ponytail. She had on a dress that flounced around her knees and a slim jacket that she'd buttoned up. She was also wearing the shoes that had danced in his memory of everything that happened Thursday night.

She smiled when she saw him, a genuine, warm smile. "Hey," she said. "You look great."

"You look better." He glanced around them. "Are you okay?"

"Me? Yep." But she was looking down when she said it, and she pretended to be studying her notes.

Ian shifted closer. He caught the scent of her perfume. "I didn't know if you'd come."

"Silly man," she said, and she looked up. "I *had* to come. I wouldn't miss this. Not after all the work I put into it."

He could add "brave" to the list of things he liked about her.

Jason popped his head out of the conference room. "There we are!" he said cheerfully. "Here's our best and brightest. Great, great—so listen, you two can watch each other's pitch if you like. Chelsea, we'll give you the ladies-first option. That okay?"

"Whatever you say, Jason," she said cheerfully, as if there were no hard feelings.

"Okay, well let's get started!"

"Yes, *let's*," she said, and she walked past Jason, her head high. He heard her wish the partners a good morning.

He followed her in and took the seat that Jason showed him to. He refused to acknowledge the wink Jason gave him, as if they were all members of a secret club they'd not let Chelsea join.

Brad Paulson smiled at Ian, too, and then looked at Chelsea. "Okay! Tesla account. Chelsea, show us what you've got."

"I'd be delighted," she said. She stood up and walked to the front of the room. "Tesla is unique in that it marries lifestyle to principle in a vehicle," she began.

Her pitch was good. Ian was impressed with her delivery—she was smooth, she was personable. She understood how to deliver the message. Ian really didn't understand why Jason had said she couldn't deliver sex appeal, because he thought she did. And he thought she had a great angle on the Tesla. In fact, as he listened to her, an idea formed in his head. When he watched her ad and watched the couple going through life in a Tesla, he saw the product in a completely different light. He and Chelsea had come at this from different angles. But one idea wasn't better than the other—they complemented each other.

Chelsea finished to a smattering of applause. "Thank you for the opportunity," she said, and she took her seat across the room from Ian.

As he got up to present his idea, he thought she gave him a smile. Maybe it was that smile, but the idea that had formed during her pitch was beginning to feel brilliant. Whatever it was, Ian completely changed the course of his life in the time it took him to walk from his seat to the front of the conference room.

Chapter 9

TO CHELSEA, IT WAS A NO-BRAINER. AS SHE watched Ian's presentation, she understood what it was that the partners loved about him. He was fantastic, his pitch sexy, catchy—all the things a campaign like this needed to be.

That didn't lessen her disappointment. She still felt wounded that her bosses would lead her on so unnecessarily as they had. She was a big girl. She could see when she'd been bested. She understood now that they'd never meant to give her Tesla, that likely they used her to light a fire under Ian to get his best work. Everyone responded to competition, didn't they?

She watched the partners eating Ian's presentation with a spoon and chocolate drizzled on top. He looked like an executive. He looked like a partner, more in tune with the world than any of the jokers sitting around that conference table.

What she had initially believed was arrogance was self-confidence. Chelsea supposed she could learn a thing or two from him about how to wear confidence. Unfortunately, she wasn't going to be here to learn anything from him.

That was the one conclusion she'd been able to reach this weekend. That was the thing that had been crystal clear to her when everything else had seemed so murky.

In all honesty, it had been a hard few days. Stuck in her studio apartment, her thoughts swimming back and forth between her feelings about what had happened with Ian, and then this pitch. She really liked Ian. Under any other scenario, she would be over the moon, wanting to see more of him. But this pitch—which represented so much more, everything she'd thought she was working toward—had tainted it.

Chelsea truly wished Ian well, but she had to stay true to herself and she could not—could *not*—let this slide. Jason and, by extension, the partners, had lied to her. They had used her. And that was not okay. Good God, she should have recognized the handwriting on the wall. So many opportunities passing her by, always a promise of next time. *You're getting there, Chelsea. Next time is yours, Chelsea.*

Ian's ad ran, and it was as good as Zimmerman had told her in line at Starbucks one afternoon. The partners began to clap, Brad Paulson most enthusiastically. Chelsea wished she'd eaten all of his Lean Cuisines.

"Great work, Ian. *Great* work," Brad said.

"Thank you," Ian said. He looked at the window for a moment. "I have put a lot of thought into this campaign. But I realize this morning it's not the right approach."

Everyone paused, including Chelsea. She stared at Ian—what was he doing?

"What do you mean?" Brad asked.

"Honestly? Now that I've seen Chelsea's ad, I think that the best approach is somewhere between the two." He was suddenly animated. "Picture this—we start with my ad. Guy in a bar, gets the girl. They drive up the PCH and we see the bra. A great image, draws in the testosterone crowd. But then," he said, moving around the table now, "we cut to babies in a very green yard with lots of flowers and bushes and trees, car seats in the Tesla sedan. It's safe, and it's safe for your children. It's a cleaner world for them too. And you see the same couple, a little older, with the kids. A flash of them, a little older still, leaving their daughter's wedding. We incorporate

Chelsea's ad. The car is safe; it handles well. It's carried them through the important parts of their life." He braced his hands against the end of the conference table. "We get the full gamut of the way Americans want to live." He stood up, spread his hands wide. "Tesla: For the way we want to live."

There was silence; Chelsea caught her breath. It was brilliant. *Really* brilliant.

"That's a *great* idea," Jason said.

"But that kind of ad only works with a team," Ian said. "You know what I'd do if I were sitting at this table? I wouldn't give this account to just one of us. It's too big. I would give it to both of us."

"Ian," Chelsea said, and she stood up. "You don't have to do this. It's okay—"

"No, no," Brad said, waving her off. "He's right; it's a great idea. You're both talented; you've both got great ideas. Tell you what—we'll mull this over," he said, looking to the other partners for agreement. "We'll have a decision by the end of the day."

Ian looked pleased with himself. He walked to the door and opened it and then waited for Chelsea, a faint smile on his face. She walked out and Ian shut the door quietly behind them.

Chelsea whirled around to him. "What the hell

are you doing? You have the account, Ian! You didn't have to do that for me—I'm okay."

"I didn't do it for you." He pointed to the door. "That was the right thing to do. It was the *smart* thing to do."

"So just like that, you give them your best idea? You didn't even take a moment to think through how something like that would work."

He leaned closer. "I didn't give them my best idea. I'm keeping that one right here," he said, tapping his finger to his breast. "What's the matter?" he asked, smiling. "Don't you want to work with me?"

"Oh, Ian." She smiled wearily. How could she explain to him that she would give anything to work with him but wouldn't? That she wanted to see where they could take this, what they could make of it, but it would never happen? "Listen, whatever happens…thank you." She moved to step around him.

"Wait, that's *it*?" he said to her, incredulous, as she began to walk away.

"For now!" she called over her shoulder. Because if she didn't keep walking, she would lose her resolve. She would give in to her desire for Ian and let Grabber-Paulson have the best of her, all for a guy.

It was ten to six when Jason called Chelsea into his office. He was sitting behind his desk, his feet propped on the edge, tossing that damn Nerf ball through the hoop. "Chelsea!" he said cheerfully. "Chel-chel! Girl of the hour!"

"Where's Ian?" she asked, expecting them both to be brought in.

"Hey, I wanted to talk to *you*," Jason said. "You were good today. Really good, Chelsea. But I wasn't surprised."

She was not going to listen to this. "Did you make your decision?" she asked.

Jason laughed. "Girl's got fire in the belly," he said cheerfully. "Yes, we've made a decision, and you're going to like it. You're going to like it a *lot*. We've decided to accept Ian's idea and give this account to *both* of you. Isn't that great? Sort of like co-chairs, right? But not really co-chairs, because someone needs the authority to sign off on stuff. We gave that to Ian. Which means *you* have all the time to work on creative. Nice, huh? It's a great idea. It's great teamwork. We're about teamwork here."

"Are we?" she asked skeptically.

Jason laughed and tossed the Nerf. Chelsea caught it and wadded it into a little ball. Jason glanced at the ball in her hand. "You can keep it," he said uncertainly. "I've got more. So. You and Ian can work out the office situation." He laughed. "We decided not to get in the way of that! Wish we had more than one, but, you know, space is limited. I'm going to reassign some of your accounts so you'll have plenty of time to work on Tesla. We're taking the final pitch to them next Tuesday." He grinned at her. "Aren't you going to say anything? You're Tesla, just like you wanted!"

Chelsea actually laughed at that. "Aren't you at least going to let me accept it?"

"Of course you accept! Why wouldn't you? It's a win-win for everyone!"

"I see why you're so good at ad work, Jason. You can spin absolutely anything. By the way, my answer is no," Chelsea said.

For once, Jason didn't seem so glib. He blinked, almost as if he hadn't heard her. "What?"

"I said, no thank you. It's been great, but I'm a big fat *no*."

"Why not?" he cried, suddenly coming to his feet. "What are you doing, Chelsea? You don't want to blow this. If you blow this, you won't get another big account—"

"*Blow* it? I never had it! You lied to me, Jason. You always lie to me. Grabber-Paulson lies to me!

You've been lying all along just to get what you wanted, and now, Ian was kind enough and wise enough to consider all the work I'd put in on this account, and you and the partners are going to dress up *his* idea and call it 'teamwork,'" she said, making invisible quotes with her fingers. "But the joke is on you because I am done with Grabber-Paulson. I've given you six great years but I won't let you walk on me anymore. I quit!"

"You can't quit!" Jason cried.

"Ha! Watch me," she said, and she turned around and walked out of his office.

"You have an employment contract!" he shouted at her.

"So sue me!" she shouted back, and she started for her cubicle. She was startled by the number of heads above their cubicle walls, having been lured out of their holes by the shouting. "Cheerio, guys! Have a nice life." She hurried to grab up the things she'd already packed and donned her coat. Only one coat—there was no time to bundle.

As she made her way to the front of the office, people were speaking to her. "Are you serious, Chelsea? Way to go, Chelsea! Did they fire you?"

But Chelsea didn't answer. She couldn't answer, for fear of losing it. And besides, she saw only one face in that crowd, and it was Ian's. He was standing in the hall just outside the partners' offices—of course Brad had been the one to tell him—with one hand on his waist, his head down, watching her.

She smiled.

He didn't. He looked very unhappy.

But Chelsea kept putting one foot in front of the other, kept forcing herself to stand up for her.

It was the hardest thing she'd ever done in her life. Not leaving a good paying job or leaving Grabber-Paulson, no—that was the easy part.

The hardest thing she'd ever done was leave a guy like Ian behind before she'd ever had a chance with him. That was the gut-wrenching, dizzy uncertainty, heartbreaking part.

Chapter 10

CHELSEA DIDN'T CHANGE OUT OF HER YOGA pants and hoodie for a week. She ate pizza and chocolate, TV-binged on classic movies and real housewives, and did absolutely nothing about finding a job. She had enough money put aside to coast for a while and her parents, thank God for them. Her father said, "You do what you need to do, honey. We're here to help."

That made Chelsea feel better, but in truth, she didn't feel very bad at all. She felt proud of herself. She had a firm belief that in standing up for herself, something good would come her way. She didn't know when or how she would find it. But she believed it with all her heart. Once she'd said no to Jason, once she'd admitted aloud what everyone knew, she'd felt nothing but relief. She'd felt as if she'd been completely honest with herself for the first time in years.

Not that it wasn't scary to walk out after six years—it was terrifying. Almost as terrifying as trusting her instincts and abilities. But nothing would ever change if Chelsea didn't take this stand; she was more certain of that every day.

She took a few calls that week—one, interestingly, from Huntson-Jones. News in advertising traveled fast, she supposed, and she had tentatively agreed to talk to them next week. But she wasn't very excited about it. The man who had called her had been effusive in his praise of her talents, had assured her that she would be a *valued team member* at Huntson-Jones. It sounded to Chelsea like more of the same.

She also heard from Marian Zarin.

"Girl, you're crazy," Marian said to her. "Everyone's talking about it. You got the Tesla account, Chelsea! Sure, you had to share it with Adonis, but still they gave it to you. Now everyone's saying you're a diva."

"But I didn't get the gig, Marian," Chelsea said. "They gave it to Ian and let him bring me along. They had already decided he was getting it, and *he* was the one who came up with the idea that I should work with him on it. People in the office are going to talk no matter what. If the partners had given it to me straight up, people in the office would say

I was aggressive. If the partners hadn't given me anything, they'd say I don't have the same charm as Ian. No matter what, they'd have something to say."

"So?" Marian demanded.

"So, I deserved the account on my own merits. But they were never going to give it to me. And they are never going to give you a big account like that, either. Name one woman in charge of a major account in that office. Just one."

Marian groaned. "Don't depress me! I already have to smell Hadeetha's lunch every day."

In the second week of unemployment, Chelsea actually changed out of her yoga pants and cleaned up the empty cartons of noodles. One afternoon she got a text from Farrah: We got Tesla account. They gave Bob your cubicle.

Bob? She groaned, thinking of *Star Wars* characters in her cubicle. But Chelsea was not surprised. She could picture Ian carrying his gym bag and a few files into his new office. She could see him leaning to the right to see the corner of Gramercy Park.

Two weeks to the day that Chelsea had quit, she awoke with renewed determination. She surfed online for jobs and found a couple that looked promising. Before she began submitting resumes, she decided to go for a run. She hadn't actually run in about six months, but it seemed as good a time as any to start up again. New life, new job, new fitness routine.

She pulled her hair into a ponytail, donned some running clothes, and jogged down the stairs of her brownstone walk-up apartment. Outside, she paused at the top of the stoop to stretch. She folded over, touching her fingers to her toes, limbering up. When she rose up again, her heart stopped.

Ian was standing at the bottom of her stoop. Why? How long had he been there? She looked up the street, almost expecting Jason to come running behind him. Or for him to hand her a manila envelope with termination papers to fill out. When he did none of those things, she said uncertainly, "Hey."

"Hey," Ian said. He shoved his hands in his back pockets, and she realized then that he was wearing jeans. It was the middle of the day, and he was dressed in jeans and sneakers and a wool coat.

"How did you…" She gestured to the brownstone and her apartment.

"Oh. You know Belinda in admin?"

Chelsea nodded; Ian shrugged.

"I see. So…why are you here? Did you come to tell me you got Tesla?"

He blinked. And then he smiled. "No. I came here to tell you I gave Tesla to Zimmerman."

"You *what*?" she almost shouted.

Ian stepped up onto the bottom step. "I didn't take it, Chelsea."

"But *why*?"

He stepped up on the next step. "Because some things are more important than big accounts."

Her heart skipped. She had told herself the very same thing. "No they aren't. I mean, *yes*, they are, but in this case—my God, Ian, why would you do that? Don't say because of me, please don't say that."

"It wasn't because of you," he said, coming up another step closer. "It was in spite of you. I quit because I agree with you, Chelsea—I don't like the way they do things." He took another step closer, and another, until he was standing on the stoop with her.

He looked so good, and Chelsea's heart began to pound in her chest.

"Can we talk about this inside?" he asked. "It's freezing."

"Sure," she said absently, and she turned around and opened the door to her apartment building. Seeing him here, so unexpectedly, was overwhelming her. It was impossible to believe that the man who had haunted her dreams and her waking thoughts for the last two weeks was *here* and had quit because of what had happened. That he'd stood up for her too.

That happened in fairy tales, not real life. Chelsea had never had a guy do anything so heroic for her.

He followed her up to her apartment. She walked inside her small space and turned around to face him as he closed the door behind them.

"I can't believe you *quit*," she said.

He chuckled and ran a hand over his head. "Yeah…neither can I. But I didn't like the way that went down. Left a bad taste in my mouth, you know?"

Oh yes, she knew.

"And it was fairly obvious to me that we are better together than apart."

She wanted to believe that, her heart ached with wanting to believe that. But Chelsea was cautious with something as delicate as her heart. "You came to that conclusion after one night?" she asked skeptically. "It seems so sudden."

"I don't know," he said with a helpless shrug. "How long is it supposed to take? I really like you, Chelsea. Maybe I am misreading the whole thing, but I had one of the best nights of my life."

Chelsea thought her heart had stopped altogether. Her lungs certainly had stopped working; she felt short of breath. No one had ever done anything like this for her. No one had ever *felt* this way about her.

"What about you?" he asked. "Did you, maybe, feel something too?"

She nodded. "I felt a lot of things. I did. But I don't know how to take this in, you standing here, you saying these things now. It's…it's a lot."

"Right," he said, and he glanced down. He shifted his weight, looking a little uncomfortable now.

"But I know this," she said. Ian's head came up. She could see the hope in his eyes and it stirred something very deep inside her.

"What's that?" he asked softly.

"I have never, in my whole life, been more turned on than I am right here, right now."

Something flared in his blue eyes. What was that passing between them, a lifetime? Love, happiness, family, adventure—everything a girl's heart yearned for? Chelsea didn't know—maybe she was confusing fairy tales with reality—but she didn't have time to think about it. She lunged for Ian at the same moment he reached for her.

He lifted her off her feet with one arm as his mouth landed on hers. He turned them around and around again, until he'd twirled them to her unmade bed. He dropped her roughly on top of it, and together, frantic, they tore at each other's clothes until they were sufficiently unclothed for what came next.

His hands found her breasts; his tongue found her mouth.

Chelsea's hands were on him, too, on warm skin, hard planes, and soft patches of ears and throat. His hands stroked every inch of her, sliding into crevices, running over her skin, and leaving streaks of lightning. He devoured her with his kiss.

"I have wanted this so much," he said as he moved down her body, settling in between her legs.

"Me too," she breathlessly agreed, and she floated away with him on a cloud of pure sensation as his tongue dipped into the flesh between her legs.

It was just as good—better—than that night in the conference room. The man was a master. He knew how to read her, knew what she wanted before she knew it herself. She shamelessly moved against him, her body having surrendered to the desire he'd shown by finding her. She sank into sexual bliss with him, shuddering with the force of it.

He slid into her then, lifting her leg up and moving deep, pushing them both to eruption.

They lay together afterward in a tangle of arms and legs, their breathing ragged. Chelsea managed to pull her hair from his mouth and rolled onto her back. Ian's hand found hers, and he wrapped his fingers tightly around it.

This was what hope felt like, Chelsea thought. She had no job, but she had never felt so hopeful. If she sat up, she was certain she would see bluebirds flitting outside her window. She giggled and looked at Ian.

He was smiling too.

"We're unemployed," she said cheerfully, and for some reason, both of them burst into laughter.

Chapter 11

"YOU DON'T GET IT," CHELSEA INSISTED TO IAN, who was patiently listening, one hip on the desk, his hands clasped before him. "She's *awful*. She's never without her phone; she forgets important details—"

"But she'll work for what we can pay her," Ian calmly pointed out. "We can't do better."

Chelsea frowned at him. He was right; he was alarmingly *always* right. And he was going to win this one. He knew it as well as she did. For extra insurance, he put his hand on her swelling belly, where their baby—highly unexpected and highly anticipated—was growing.

"It's going to be all right," he assured her.

"You always say that," she said crossly.

"Have I been wrong?"

Chelsea looked around at their little storefront office in Park Slope. "No," she admitted, and she teasingly punched his shoulder. "Just don't say I didn't warn you." She pushed his hand from her belly so she could move closer to kiss him.

"I promise. I will never say you didn't warn me any more than I will say I told you so. Which, you know, I could say a *lot*."

She couldn't help but laugh at that. It was true. She was overly cautious with their fledgling business.

They'd made the plunge a year ago. They'd opened their advertising firm and had begun with the pizzeria around the corner. Radio, print— sales had gone up, and the next thing they knew, they had a regional insurance company, a car lot, and a nanny service. It wasn't much, and it sure wasn't the big national accounts they were both used to, but it was a start. And it was their work, their vision.

Currently, they had a few bids out. They'd just moved into an apartment a few blocks away. They had a fantastic life together, and they were happy.

Pure, unadulterated happiness.

"I'm going to call Farrah now and give her the good news."

"Better you than me," Chelsea muttered.

He smiled and kissed her forehead. "I'm going to invite her to the wedding too."

"Well for heaven's sake, Ian, why don't you ask her if she'll be our nanny?"

He arched one gold brow. "Hey…"

"Don't even," she warned him, and she smiled. "I'm going to go pick up some lunch. How about Thai?"

Ian sighed and took a seat at his desk. "I will be so happy when that baby is born and we can get off the eat-around-the-world track."

"Yes or no?" Chelsea asked, resting her hand on her belly.

Ian smiled at her. "Yes. Whatever you want, Chels. You know that."

Yes, she knew that.

"While you're out, pick up some more Lean Cuisine," he said, and he grabbed her bottom, giving it an affectionate squeeze.

She went out onto the street and looked up at the crystalline blue sky. She thought she'd never seen it so blue.

She and Ian were a study of nevers. They'd never seen a blizzard like the one that trapped them in the Grabber-Paulson suite. They'd never walked out on good paying jobs. Ian had told her he'd never thought he'd be this guy, the family guy, that he'd never even known he wanted it.

And Chelsea? Chelsea had never realized a love

could run so deep that hope could buoy a person so completely.

She'd never been so happy.

the
Bridesmaid

A NOVELLA

Chapter 1

IT WAS BAD ENOUGH THAT THE DRESS WAS A poufy plantation ball gown number, complete with a sash and apron in a disturbing shade of peach, but it also wouldn't fit in Kate's suitcase. Which meant she was going to have to carry it on the plane. Which she had explained to Lisa when they'd shopped for the bridesmaid gowns six months ago.

"But I *love* it!" Lisa had said, and had made Kate turn around one more time on the little pedestal in the bridal salon.

It was puzzling to Kate. Lisa was her cousin and her best friend. She was pretty and so very stylish. Kate had always wished she were as stylish as Lisa. She'd always admired the way Lisa went after things she wanted, her generosity and kindness, her fabulous sense of humor. But Kate did not care for the way Lisa tended to flip out at the first sign of pressure, or the way she'd latched on to a vision for her wedding that defied logic.

Lisa wanted a plantation wedding. In Seattle. And of course Lisa had bought a slinky mermaid wedding gown for herself. But for her sister Lori, and Kate, her maid of honor, she'd insisted on the peach monstrosities, with clunky platform shoes. Plus, she had the most appalling idea that Kate and Lori would wear their hair in French twists from which peach ribbons would cascade. "Like morning mist," Lisa had said dreamily.

"Like morning puke," Kate's little sister Cassidy had bluntly countered.

Kate had complained to her mother, whose sister had given birth to Lisa and Lori. But Kate's mother was only mildly sympathetic. "It's Lisa's wedding. If she wants that kind of dress, she can have it. When you get married, you can make her wear purple or something."

As there was no prospect of that in sight for Kate, revenge purple didn't seem like a real option.

"And besides, I happen to like peach," her mother had added.

Kate hated the dress, but this morning, she hated it with a passion so strong she might have launched missiles, because she couldn't even get the damn thing into the garment bag—the *pink* garment bag—for the flight from New York to Seattle. It was too poufy.

Kate glanced at the clock; she had an hour before a car arrived to whisk her off to the airport. She still had *so* many things to do. She was not the most organized person on the planet.

She was shoving another pair of shoes into her suitcase when her cell phone rang. "Hi, Mother," she said, hurrying to turn down the TV blaring in the background. "Can't talk long, a car is coming."

"I was calling to see if your flight was on time."

"Yep," Kate said as she frantically sorted through her jewelry box. At least she thought the flight was on time—she hadn't gotten any alerts on her phone. "Why?"

"I'm worried about that storm."

"Storm? What storm?" Kate turned around to her TV. The weatherman was gesturing to a big swath of purple across the middle of the country. It was nowhere near New York. "Are you talking about that?" Kate asked, pointing to a TV her mother couldn't see. "That's Kansas. Or Missouri. One of those corn states."

"It's a huge late-season snowstorm between you and us. Everything is shut down. It's global warming, you know. Greenhouse emissions."

Every inch of rain, every snowflake was now

classified as global warming by Kate's mother. Nevertheless, the storm was not in New York. "It's okay," Kate said impatiently. "They'll just fly over or around it. Not to worry, Mom! I'm on my way!"

"I hope so. It would be devastating if the maid of honor didn't make it. Lisa would explode and die, I think. And it seems like every time you fly home, something happens."

"I have flown home once since I moved to New York, and there was a thirty-minute delay. That's just part of flying these days." Kate had moved to New York six months ago to take a job as an assistant editor at a big publishing house. It was a dream job for an English major. Kate had dreamed of being in publishing since high school, when she'd read *A Clockwork Orange*. Until that book, she hadn't understood how lyrical and powerful storytelling could be, and after that book, she wanted to be a part of it. The pay for assistant editors sucked, but Kate loved it. Loved it, loved it, loved it. And she loved New York. "Listen, I really have to go," she said.

"We'll see you at the airport. Have a safe flight, honey."

Kate clicked off and threw her phone and charger in her purse. And then, through some miracle of physics, managed to shove the bridesmaid dress into the hanging bag, which ballooned to twice its size. Kate cursed Lisa once more, slung her tote bag over her shoulder, wrangled the unwieldy garment bag under her arm, and began to lug her suitcase down to the street from her third-floor walk-up.

―◦◦◦―

Missy Weaten gave Joe a kiss on the cheek. "Call me when you get back to New York, okay?"

"You bet," Joe said, and half fell, half stood from her car at the train station. Bleary-eyed, he watched her as she drove away. He wondered what exactly had happened last night between them. He was fairly certain nothing had, given his high state of inebriation several hours ago, but then again, he was Joe Firretti. He was a red-blooded man, and when opportunity presented itself—even when Missy Weaten presented herself—sometimes, things happened.

He noticed an elderly couple staring at him. He gave them a half smile, ran his fingers through his hair, then straightened his suit coat. He pulled his bag behind him into the train station.

He was not really the type to get wasted the way he had last night. But his pals from work had taken him out for a spectacular send-off. He was on his way to a new job, a fantastic job. A job that came along once in a lifetime. Joe knew it. The financial firm where he worked knew it. The financial firm in Seattle that had extended the very generous offer of employment knew it. Joe would be heading up the technology side of a major international bank.

He had not intended to leave quite this soon for Seattle, but then the bank's head honcho had flown in from Switzerland, and they'd told Joe it was imperative that he meet the CEO while he was available. So Joe had moved his departure up a week. He'd put a deposit down on an apartment and had arranged to have his things picked up and moved to Seattle the next week.

Hoozah.

He stepped up to the ticket machine, rubbed his face with his hands, and glanced at his watch. He had three hours before his plane left, plenty of time to get to Newark and get through security.

He bought his ticket, made his way down to the train, and climbed on board. He wished he'd eaten something. Last night had been a whirl of bars and restaurants and blonde women and no food that he recalled. He hoped he hadn't said anything to Missy to make her think that after two years of her coming on to him, he'd changed his mind. Just to make sure, he'd email her later and thank her for the send-off, then move on.

He was moving on; yes, he was. That's what Joe wanted. He was almost 99 percent sure that's what he wanted. He knew he wanted a bigger opportunity, something great. He knew he wanted to advance in his career. He wanted...*something*. Something. Joe wasn't quite sure what it was, but he felt as close to "it" as he ever had.

At Newark, he made his way into the airport in the middle of a great blob of humanity. Jesus, it was crowded. He maneuvered his way up to the airline kiosk, past grandmas with their belly bags, past crying babies and little kids who ran without looking, past harried business travelers like him.

When he reached the kiosk, he punched the screen as he had a thousand times before, going quickly through the required entries. Something pink was in his peripheral vision, darting in and out, in and out. He glanced at the kiosk directly to his right and saw a woman with shoulder-length blonde hair, an enormous suitcase, and an even larger pink garment bag. At least he thought it was a garment bag. It was hard to make out; it was bloated and huge and reminded him of a life raft.

She was trying to hold on to all of it as she used one finger to jab at the screen.

Joe pulled out his license and held it up to the airline attendant. She handed him his boarding pass. "The flight is delayed about an hour," she said. "Gate 12."

"No, come on," Joe whined. "Not today. I had a late night last night, and the last thing I want is to be hanging out in a crowded airport with all of them," he said, jerking his thumb over his shoulder. He smiled at the attendant.

She did not return his smile. "It's better than listening to people complain about it all day, trust me. A big storm is cutting across the country. A lot of flights have been canceled. Honestly? You'll be lucky to get out."

"Great," Joe muttered. He sighed, took the boarding pass, and moved away from the kiosk. He inadvertently stepped on the giant pink raft when he did.

"Hey!" the woman said.

"Sorry," Joe muttered and shimmied around her, the pink raft, and the blue bag that looked as if it could hold a small house.

After an interminable wait in the security line, Joe fit his belt back through the loops of his pants, returned his shoes to his feet, and wandered through the terminal, looking for a coffee shop. He ordered a cup of joe, black and thick. He downed it, then collapsed into a chair at the gate. He leaned back, intending to doze, when something knocked against the back of his head. He sat up with a start and turned around, just in time to see that pink raft go sailing by. What had gotten him was the woman's tote bag, draped over her shoulder.

Unbelievable.

Joe stood up and went in search of a calmer place to nap before his plane left.

He found a place, but his nap was a fitful one, due to all the announcements of cancellations and delays. Still, Joe felt a little better when he woke later and stretched out his legs and his arms above his head. He squinted at his gate; they were boarding. Hallelujah—he'd get out of this pit after all. He sauntered to the boarding line, maneuvering once again through even more clumps of people. It almost seemed as if they were being pumped into the airport in groups of twos and threes.

He was among the first to board, thanks to his frequent flyer miles, and settled in to an aisle seat on the same aisle as an elderly woman who had her attention turned to the window. The flight attendant announced to those coming onboard that the flight was completely full and to quickly take their seats. Must be some storm, Joe thought absently, and flipped through the SkyMall catalog.

He was sure another person could not squeeze

onto that plane when he saw the pink raft inch its way on board. He watched as the woman and a flight attendant worked to shove the raft into the tiny garment closet. It took both of them and a lot of discussion, but finally, they managed to get the raft in and get the door shut.

The woman was smiling when she stopped at Joe's row. "I think that's my seat," she said, pointing to the middle seat.

What were the odds? "Sure," Joe said and stood up to allow her to pass.

Her big tote bag knocked into him as she shimmied into the row.

It seemed to take her an inordinate amount of time to get situated, trying her bag beneath the seat in front of her in various configurations, then finally using both boots to push it under.

And then she started to chat.

"Whew," she said. "This is one crowded flight."

He did not respond. It was his experience that the less he said, the less people tried to talk to him, as he really had no desire to make friends on every flight he took. He preferred to be left alone, to work or sleep or listen to music if he wanted.

But the chick sitting next to him, cute though she was with her bright green eyes and silky blonde hair, *talked*. She said, apparently to no one, that she didn't like to fly, but that she had to get to a wedding. When that elicited no response, she asked Joe why he was on his way to Seattle.

"Job."

"Job!" she said and nodded as if she approved. "What sort of job?"

"Computers." God, was there any way to cut this off without being a complete jerk? Joe realized he suddenly had a raging headache.

"You will love Seattle. I'm from there. It doesn't rain as much as you think—it can be really nice."

He hadn't said one word about rain. "Okay."

"It's really beautiful."

"Yeah… I've been a few times."

"Oh. Okay." She settled back, helping herself to the armrest between them.

"Gooooood afternoon, ladies and gentlemen," said a voice over the intercom. "We've got some light turbulence ahead associated with this big blizzard that's cutting across the country. We're going to ask the flight attendants to remain in their seats until we feel it's safe for them to be up and around. In the meantime, please stay in your seats with your seat belts fastened until we turn off the seat-belt sign."

"But I'm starving. I wanted peanuts," the woman next to him muttered.

The pilot said some other things that were lost on Joe because he had closed his eyes and was drifting off again. He apparently drifted hard, because he was only vaguely aware of takeoff. He didn't know how long he dozed, but he was rudely awakened by a rather severe drop in altitude that caused everyone in the cabin to cry out.

"Folks, we're heading into some turbulence. Please stay in your seats with your seat belts securely fastened," the pilot said again, which was reiterated by the more urgent voice of the flight attendant.

Joe sat up and glanced to his left. The woman in the center seat had a mound of little peanut bags on her tray. She noticed him looking at them and picked one up. "You want one? They came by while you were snoring."

"I was snoring?" he asked, mortified.

"A little." She shook the peanut bag at him again. "You want?"

"No. Thanks."

She shrugged and, with one hand, swiped the peanuts into her bag and lifted her tray table.

At the same moment, they hit another pocket of turbulence that made the plane shake. The woman grabbed the armrest, her eyes wide. "What the hell?"

"It's just turbulence," Joe said with the authority

of a seasoned traveler, but he was wondering the same thing. That was a pretty big drop.

"Hey, folks, I've got some news," the pilot's disembodied voice said above them. "What we've got here is the convergence of a Canadian cold front and a tropical storm coming up from the Atlantic that's just creating havoc across the country. Unfortunately, this big late-season blizzard had some pretty impressive ice associated with it, and we have an instrument that's acting a little wacky. We're going to land in Dallas and have a look."

"Oh no," the woman muttered, her head bouncing back against the seat back. "No, no, no, *no*. I *have* to be in Seattle."

No, Joe silently agreed.

"Don't worry, we're going to get you to Seattle," the pilot said, apparently able to hear the hue and cry that was welling up in the cabin. "But we want to get you there safely."

"I don't care how you get me there," she muttered. "Just *get* me there."

Chapter 2

FROM THE SMALL SLIVER OF WINDOW THAT KATE could see, it looked as if every plane flying across the United States had diverted to Dallas. Beneath slate gray skies, planes of all sizes were lined up on the tarmac, waiting for available gates.

They'd been waiting for two hours. Two excruciatingly long hours in which she'd been squeezed in between a grandma with generous hips and a man with impossibly broad shoulders. With the latter, Kate was engaged in a silent battle for the armrest. Every time she moved, he popped his elbow onto it. Every time he turned around to look for the flight attendant—which was often—she reclaimed it. What was it about men that made them think they had some inalienable right to the armrests?

He sighed again, loudly and with great exasperation, and then kicked his feet around under the seat in front of him like a little boy who had grown frustrated that he could not find a comfortable position.

Kate rolled her eyes, opened her purse, and took out a bag of peanuts.

His attention snapped instantly to her.

She opened the bag, fished out one peanut, and popped it into her mouth.

He was riveted.

Kate ate another peanut and glanced at him from the corner of her eye.

His gaze narrowed; his vivid blue eyes zeroed in on hers, silently challenging. Kate munched her peanuts and considered him. He was cute, she thought. Dark, wavy hair, long enough to tuck behind his ears. Sexy lips. Yep, he was so cute that Kate momentarily forgot he was an armrest hog.

His gaze fell to her bag of peanuts, and then to her purse.

"Would you like some?" Kate asked pleasantly.

He clenched his jaw. He was trying very hard not to want them, she could see that, and she couldn't help but smile brightly. "I have several bags."

"Maybe that's why they ran out of bags for everyone else a half hour ago."

"Testy," she said with a shrug and ate another peanut. "My philosophy is, you snooze, you lose. In your case, literally." She laughed at her own joke, then reached into her purse and rummaged around, finding another bag. She held it up. "Do you want one… Wait, what did you say your name was?"

"I didn't," he said tightly.

She wiggled the bag of peanuts.

"*Joe*," he said.

"I'm Kate." She smiled and handed him the bag. "Knock yourself out."

"Thanks," he said, and when he lifted his arm to take the bag from her, Kate firmly planted her elbow on the armrest.

He tore the bag open, tipped it upside down, and dumped all the peanuts in his mouth. One would think they'd been on the plane without food for days instead of hours.

He'd just wadded the empty wrapper into a tight little ball when the engines suddenly fired. Cries of relief went up from the cabin as the plane shuddered forward. The captain, Kate noticed, didn't say anything. He was sick of it too.

The plane slid up to a gate, and although the flight attendant instructed the passengers to remain seated with their seat belts fastened until the captain had turned off the illuminated sign, no one listened. There was a mad push to get off that plane, a lot of shouting for people to hurry up. Joe popped up from his seat instantly. He was cute *and* tall, an

inch or two over six feet, Kate thought. He was also
trim and muscular, and looked as if he did a lot of
working out.

He blocked the aisle, gesturing impatiently for
Kate and the grandma to get out too.

"Oh! *Thank* you," Kate said gratefully and hurried forward to rescue her bridesmaid dress, which
took some wresting out of the tiny space, much
to the annoyance of everyone behind her. Once
Kate had freed it, she hoisted the thing on her back
and slugged her tote bag over her shoulder. She
marched forward, anxious to be as far from that
plane as she could get.

Unfortunately, the plane disgorged its passengers into an overcrowded terminal dripping with
bad mojo and body odor. In the melee of angry
passengers and harried airline personnel shouting
at everyone to calm down, Kate lost sight of Joe.
She thought she spotted him on the other side of
the airline desk helping the grandma into a seat, but
the swelling crowd quickly obstructed Kate's view.

And really, she had other pressing issues on her
mind at that moment: a bathroom. She fought her
way across the wide corridor from the gate to stand
in line at the women's bathroom with what felt like
another person on her back and a bowling ball in
her shoulder bag.

Several minutes later, when she emerged once again into the terminal, it seemed, impossibly, as if things were even more chaotic. She was dismayed to see the number of cancellations on the arrivals and departures board. Lisa was going to have a complete meltdown if Kate was delayed. Her cousin was not exactly the most laid-back woman in the world.

The attendant at the airline desk was making an announcement, but Kate couldn't make out a word she was saying. So she pushed her way through the crowd and found herself next to a very thin, very put-together blonde. The blonde's fingers were flying across her phone.

"Excuse me," Kate said. "Sorry to bother you, but did you happen to hear what they said?"

"Yes," the woman said without looking up. "We are to collect our baggage and they will try and re-route us." She suddenly looked up. "But don't get your hopes up. The news is reporting that the air traffic controllers are going on strike at midnight."

"Wait, *what*?" Kate exclaimed, completely startled by that news and the fact that a mass of humanity had turned around and was starting to move in one fleshy wall toward the baggage claim.

"You haven't heard?" Blondie asked. "Big freak blizzard across one half the country, and air traffic controllers are about to strike. We're screwed."

"Oh no," Kate said. "I cannot be screwed. I *can't*. I have to be at a wedding!"

"If I were you, I'd see about getting a hotel around here somewhere. I don't think anyone is going anywhere. Good luck," she added and put herself in the people stream to baggage claim.

This could not be happening. Lisa would flip out, and Kate really didn't want to live the rest of her life and possibly die at DFW airport. She frantically dug in her bag for her phone as she moved with the wall of people toward baggage claim.

At the baggage carousel, Kate was able to prop up her pink garment bag to stand directly beside her so that she could call Lisa. *"Hey!"* she said brightly when Lisa answered. "How's the bride?"

"Where *are* you?" Lisa demanded. "I've been trying to get hold of you all day!"

"You have?" Kate asked. "I'm on my way—"

"Oh God, that's right," Lisa sighed. "I forgot you were flying in today. I just really need to talk to you," she said. "I don't…something is going on."

Lisa clearly had not heard about the storm or the impending strike, Kate thought, which was good. But she didn't need any additional drama right now. "What's up?" she asked reluctantly.

"I don't know if I want to do this," Lisa said. "Is that awful?"

"Do what?" Kate asked and was knocked from the back as an impatient man went barreling past her. She managed to catch herself and her dress.

"*Get married,*" Lisa said impatiently. "I mean, I love him, at least I think I do, but honestly, sometimes I wonder if I really, truly know what love is, Kate! What if there is someone else out there who is a better match? How do I know for certain that Kiefer is the one?"

Lord. Kate was not alarmed; she was annoyed. Lisa had always been like this, always creating drama, always second-guessing everything about her life. Kate's aunt—Lisa's mom—said she was a dreamer. Kate's mom said Lisa was a little wishy-washy. Kate thought Lisa was just straight-up nuts most of the time, with a little deranged thrown in to make things interesting. "Are you kidding, Lisa? Your wedding is in two days. Two days!"

"I know, I know," Lisa moaned. "But we had this discussion last night—well, more of a fight, really. Anyway, he said there were certain things I ought to understand by now, and I said, sometimes I think I understand too much, and he said, what's *that* supposed to mean—"

The baggage carousel suddenly cranked to life, drowning out Lisa's recounting of the fight.

"Okay, listen," Kate said. "You have to take a

breath. I'll be there soon, okay? You're just having bridal jitters, that's all. Everyone gets them. But, Lisa, do *not* flip out. Do you understand? Don't flip out! Don't do anything stupid until I get there."

"Okay," Lisa said, but she didn't sound particularly on board with that plan.

"Is that a promise?"

"Sort of."

"Okay, well look, I'll call you in a few hours. Right now, I have to go. I have to…change planes," Kate said quickly.

"Call me as soon as you can," Lisa demanded.

She would call her all right, Kate thought. If she lugged this damn Scarlett O'Hara dress across a freak snowstorm and an air traffic controller strike for nothing, she could not be held responsible for what she would do to her most beloved cousin and best friend.

She spotted her suitcase coming around. Naturally, it was on top of other bags. She pushed her way into the rail, then muscled her heavy bag off the merry-go-round. She knew she shouldn't have brought so many shoes.

With her belongings all around her now, and the dress propped up beside her, Kate pondered what she should do next.

"What is that, anyway, your own personal flotation device?" a male voice asked.

Kate had to lean forward and around her garment bag to see her ex-seatmate. Joe looked completely unruffled by all the airport drama. At his foot was a gray suitcase, only half the size of hers. "One can never be too prepared, I always say," Kate said. "Where's yours?"

He actually smiled at that. "If I am going to be some place that requires a personal flotation device, I don't think my flotation device is going to make much of a difference."

Kate smiled. "You make a good argument. So did you hear? Air traffic controller strike is coming."

"I heard," he said. "So maybe you do have the right idea," he said, looking at her garment bag. "Because if that happens, the only way out of Dallas might be via raft."

"Hey!" a woman said behind her.

Kate turned around to see Blondie standing next to her, still furiously typing away on her phone, two bags stacked neatly beside her. "So some people are trying to get to Austin or Houston from here to see if they can get out. They're further south and can route around the storm through Phoenix or someplace like that."

"Oh," Kate said. She was aware that Joe had suddenly moved closer, was standing at her back, listening. "How are they getting there?"

"Rental cars," Blondie said and looked up. "Just down that hall."

"Thank you," Kate said. "Did you get one?"

"Not me. I am checking into the Gaylord and getting a massage. You should really do the same."

"I'll think about it," Kate said. She did not relish the thought of driving to Austin or Houston, not without at least seeing what the airline came up with. But neither did she like the idea of leaving the airport to check into a hotel. She turned around to speak to Joe, but he was gone—she spotted him striding in the direction of the rental car agencies. Apparently he thought that was the only way out of here, and the fact that he did made an impression on Kate. Maybe he knew something she didn't know.

She gathered up her mélange of luggage and hurried after him.

Joe was in the Dollar Rent A Car line, so Kate went to the Budget line, determined to get a car before he did. But as she waited, she noticed that voices were getting louder and louder at her counter. People in front of her were sighing loudly and with frustration, muttering under their breath.

She checked Joe's position at Dollar and was

startled to see him looking at her. She quickly looked away. The couple in front of her suddenly whirled about with stormy expressions. "Is something wrong?" Kate asked.

"They don't have any cars!" the woman said angrily. "I can*not* believe they don't have any cars! They are a *car rental company*," she said emphatically.

"No one has any cars," said a man behind Kate. "They've all been grabbed."

"Then why don't they bring them from other places?" the woman demanded, as if it were perfectly reasonable to expect that the car rental agency could have anticipated this disaster.

Kate began to gather her things. It was back to the airline, she guessed. "I heard that Hertz had a few cars," the man behind her said.

That brought Kate's head up. She whipped around to look at the Hertz counter, and when she did, she noticed Joe was looking at her again. His gaze followed hers to the Hertz counter. And then he looked at her again.

Kate suddenly lurched in the direction of Hertz, dragging her garment bag and kicking her tote bag in front of her until she could dip down and pick it up as she sprinted across the tile floor. By the time she had picked it up, however, Joe had made an acrobatic leap over the blue rope of Dollar Rent A

Car and was sprinting ahead of her in the direction
of Hertz.

Kate angrily used her garment bag as a blocker
and actually rushed through a couple deep in conversation to shorten the distance she had to cover
to beat Joe. But she was weighed down with her
things, and he obviously possessed some freakish
natural athletic talent, because he didn't even look
winded as he sailed to a spot in line in front of her.
He turned around and smiled at her. "Sorry, but I
have to get to Seattle."

"So do I!" she said sternly. "I have to get to
a wedding!"

"And I have to get to the opportunity of a lifetime. It's every man for himself."

"That is *not* fair!" Kate cried.

"Who said natural disasters were fair?" He
smiled at her.

"Do *not* smile at me," she said angrily. "Do.
Not. *Smile.*"

But he did smile. He smiled with twinkly blue
eyes as if she amused him, as if they were standing
at some bar in the middle of happy hour instead of a
crowded airport in the middle of a natural disaster.

And then the Armrest Hog got the last rental car
at DFW.

Chapter 3

THE CAR JOE GOT WAS ROUGHLY THE SIZE OF A pickle jar. He couldn't make the driver's seat go back far enough to accommodate his legs and cursed the idiot who had designed such a stupidly small vehicle.

The guy at the counter had told him Austin had one airport, but Houston had two. Joe had instantly concluded that his odds of getting a flight out had to double with two airports. "How long will it take me to get to Houston?" he asked.

"Three and a half hours on a good day," the man had said.

"Okay. How long on a stupendously bad day?"

The man had laughed. "Have a good trip, sir!" he'd said cheerfully as he handed Joe the keys.

"Too late for that," Joe had muttered and had stomped out of the office with the keys in hand.

After he'd wedged himself in the car and started

driving—directly into the sun, that was—he was reminded that he had a splitting headache, and after a day of trying to sober up, he was ravenously hungry. In fact, he was surfing his phone for any nearby McDonald's as traffic crawled along, which resulted in him taking a wrong turn.

When Joe looked up, he realized he had just entered the river of vehicles moving at a snail's pace into the terminal. "Ah hell," he muttered, then pounded the steering wheel a few times to let off some frustration.

Traffic into the terminal was barely moving as people drove in to pick up stranded passengers. Joe's fingers drummed impatiently on the steering wheel. He tried to find a radio station, but everyone was talking about the blizzard and the impending strike. He switched that off, then turned his head slightly to shove fingers through his hair. That's when he caught sight of pink in his peripheral vision. He sat up; he could see her on the sidewalk, taking up an entire bench with her pink raft and luggage. Kate herself was sitting with her knees together, her elbows braced against them, her head in her hands, her blonde hair spilling around her shoulders.

"Good luck," he sighed as he inched by. But as he neared the split in the road—right would take him to freedom, away from the terminal, while left would circle back around—he inexplicably went left.

"What are you *doing*?" he shouted at himself. Yes, okay, he'd taken pity on her. For one thing, she was pretty with those eyes and that hair. He had a thing for silky hair. And in spite of the fact that she had no spatial awareness when it came to shared armrests, she seemed nice. After all, she'd given him a bag of peanuts. Last, he had to acknowledge that she was severely handicapped with that pink thing. The least he could do was give her a ride to Houston.

"Consider it your good deed of the day," he muttered to himself as he maneuvered into the lane to pick up passengers. "If you do this good deed, you won't feel too bad when you grab the last seat on some flight to Seattle."

It took another ten minutes to reach the curb. She was now sitting up, her shapely legs, encased in boots and tights, sprawled before her, her head back on the bench and her eyes closed. Joe rolled down the window. "Hey, Kate!" he called out the window.

She sat up with a start and looked wildly about. Joe honked his horn. "Kate! Over here!"

She realized where he was and stood up, squinting at him warily. "*Joe?*"

"I'm going to Houston. Want to come?"

Now she looked completely suspicious, as if she

thought it was some sort of joke, as if someone was going to leap out from behind a bush and announce that she'd been punked. So much for good intentions, Joe thought.

"I just thought I'd offer. But you don't have to go—"

"No!" Kate did a funny little hop. "I mean *yes*! *Yesssss!*"

Now Joe was the one who was startled. She was suddenly dragging her things toward the car. He hopped out and hurried around to help her. "Here," she said, shoving her suitcase at him.

That thing was heavy—what was she carrying, a bunch of bricks? "What is in here?" he asked, lugging it along to the car.

"Shoes," she said breathlessly. "And books."

Joe threw it into the trunk and closed it. Kate was trying to get the pink thing in the backseat. He walked around, intending to help her. "Let me help you."

"Got it!" she said quickly. "It can't get wrinkled." She bent into his car, squirming around as she tried to fit the thing in perfectly.

But the only thing Joe could see was her derriere. He didn't mean to look, but come on, how could her help it? He was a guy, and *that* was a nice derriere. When she'd finally situated the pink raft as she wanted, she backed out, turned around, and looked up at him, pushing her hair back from her face. There was a slender moment when her gaze flicked over his face, and then her eyes narrowed slightly.

She knew he'd been looking.

"What's in there, anyway?" he asked.

"In there? In there is the ugliest, most hideous, god-awful poufy piece of peach taffeta in the history of mankind. But I have to wear it or my cousin will *die*. And I'm not kidding."

Joe smiled. "Okay, then. Let's get out of here, huh?"

"Please," she said primly and slid very gracefully into the passenger seat of that stupidly small car, and stuffed her shoulder bag in at her feet.

Joe walked around and wedged himself in again, then eased in front of another car.

"I thought we could grab something to eat on the way out," he said. "I don't know about you, but I'm starving."

"Oh, me too!" she said, sinking back into the passenger seat. "I tried to get some yogurt at the food court, but there is nothing left. Nothing! It's like zombies went through and ate everything."

"Zombies don't eat," he said absently as he pulled into traffic.

She looked at him as if she thought he was crazy. "What do you mean, they don't eat?"

"Zombies are dead," he said. "They don't eat. Haven't you ever seen a zombie movie?"

"No."

"No?" Joe had never known a single person who hadn't seen a zombie movie, with the exception of his mother. It was practically a requirement for his generation, which he assumed Kate was part of. "You have to see a zombie movie. Just one. You can't go an entire lifetime without it," he said as they began to inch out of the terminal.

She laughed. "I've made it twenty-eight years without seeing one."

Yeah, well, he would keep his opinions about that to himself. "So how are you at navigating?" he asked and thrust the one-page map the rental counter had given him in her direction.

She snatched it out of his hand and peered closely. "I happen to be pretty fantastic at navigating. Where are we?"

He pointed to the terminal and the highway they'd be entering. Which they did, about fifteen minutes later, and began to zip along at a top speed of sixty-five miles per hour.

They hadn't gone far when Joe spied the Golden Arches. He veered off the highway and turned into McDonald's.

Kate looked up. Her mouth dropped open. "Wait—you're not going *here*, are you?"

"Yep," he said and pulled into a parking spot. "I'm hungry, remember?"

"But not McDonald's!"

"What's wrong with Mickey D's?" Joe asked as he unbuckled his seat belt. He knew full well what was wrong with it—he'd had enough girlfriends to know that the nutritional values of the food were not in the acceptable range for sleek New York women.

"You're kidding, right?"

"No."

She gasped. "Calories! Fat!"

He was too hungry to debate it. "You don't look like you have to worry about that," he said gruffly. "And, besides, we don't have time for a fine dining experience, remember? So—are you hungry?"

Kate shifted forward and squinted out the front windshield at the restaurant. "Starving," she muttered and unbuckled her seat belt.

A few minutes later, they were in the car again. Kate, Joe noticed, was wolfing down the burger she'd disdained. She happened to come up for breath and noticed his look of amusement. "Don't judge me," she warned him and punctuated that with a big bite of burger.

Joe laughed. He liked a woman who could eat.

"Bon appétit," he said as he started the car up and backed out of the parking space.

Kate had polished off the burger and the fries she'd bought by the time they neared downtown Dallas and a dizzying display of highways in the sky, looping up and over each other. Just as they began to enter that mess, her phone rang.

"Don't answer it," Joe said. "I'm not sure what road I'm supposed to take."

"45," she said and bent over, digging through her bag.

"Come on, call them back," he pleaded, but Kate already had the phone in hand.

"Lisa!" she said cheerfully. "What's up?"

"I don't see it. I don't see 45," he said.

Kate pointed out the front window. *"Left,"* she whispered, and Joe wondered if she truly thought that was even remotely helpful.

"Oh, did you hear? Yes, well, not to worry. I'm on my way to Houston right now. Supposedly, planes are still flying out of Houston. Huh? Oh, it's close. Like an hour or something."

"It's at least three hours," Joe said.

Kate waved her hand at him in a manner that Joe believed meant he was not to talk.

"45," he said to her. "Where is it?"

"That's another passenger," Kate said into the

phone. "Lisa, can you hold on one minute?" She covered the phone with her hand. "45 is a left exit. *Left!* And it says Houston in big white letters."

"You don't have to be sarcastic," he grumbled and began the arduous task of slipping a tiny little car across five lanes of much faster and much thicker traffic. The sign, he noticed, did not say Houston.

"So I'll be there in plenty of time—" She paused. She bent her head, rubbed her forehead. "Okay, what did he say?" she asked and listened attentively. After a few moments, she nodded and said, "Okay, listen, Lisa. Listen to me. Getting married is a big deal. He is probably just a little nervous, right? I mean, he wouldn't have asked you to marry him if he didn't love you and didn't want to spend the rest of his life with you."

"Not necessarily," Joe said.

Kate gasped and jerked her wide-eyed gaze to him.

He shrugged. "I'm just saying," he said casually. "Sometimes, women will put unbelievable pressure on a guy to put a ring on it."

Kate's brows suddenly dipped. She pressed a finger to her lips, and said, "He's kidding. And who is he, anyway? But I know Kiefer, and I know he is crazy about you." She glared at Joe once more. "What?" she suddenly cried. "God, Lisa, can you please not do anything crazy until I get there? Please? You always do this when you get stressed. You freak out about things that aren't even real and make a mess! I will be there in less than twelve hours!" she said.

Joe looked at her and winced a little. He thought she might be overselling things a little.

But Kate glared again and pointed at him and mouthed the words, *Not a word.*

"Okay, thank you," Kate said into the phone. "Go get a massage or something. Just chill out. Relax. Where is Mom, anyway?"

Kate stayed on the phone another couple of minutes, and finally hung up. When she did, she tossed her phone into her bag, folded her arms, and stared at him.

Joe felt a prickly bit of heat under his collar. "What?"

"You know what."

"I was just saying—"

"You don't say that to a bride forty-eight hours before her wedding!" Kate exclaimed, her hands moving wildly. "You don't know her—she's nuts. She can make mountains out of tiny little anthills without as much as a match."

That made absolutely no sense, but Joe wasn't going to point that out. "So what did the groom say?" he asked.

Kate moaned and sank back in her seat. "That he was feeling antsy," she said. "Whatever that means."

Joe knew exactly what it meant. "It means he is feeling antsy. That's it. I mean, think about it—he has to put on a monkey suit and stand up before a bunch of people and say things he wouldn't say to his best friend, you know? That would make any guy antsy." He should know. He once came dangerously close to it himself. Sort of close. He hadn't actually asked Mona to marry him, but he'd *thought* about it, and just thinking about it had made him antsy.

"That's ridiculous. If you love someone, you ought to be able to say it. Like a grown-up."

"I am sure he can *say* it," Joe said. "Like a grown-up. But why does he have to say it in a monkey suit?"

"Ohmi—Forget it. Men are so alike," she muttered and looked out her window.

"Oh, and women aren't?" he asked. "And by the way, while you were convincing your friend with cold feet to go ahead and take the plunge, you were not navigating. The sign we just passed said Tyler. Would you please look and tell me how far to Tyler?"

"Tyler?" she repeated and dug out the map. She studied it a moment, then glanced at him. "We're going the wrong way."

"Wrong way!" he said disbelievingly.

"We should be going south, not east."

Joe slapped his hand against the wheel. "Holy—"

"You were supposed to get on 45. Why didn't you get on 45? The sign said Houston; I don't know how you missed it."

"I wasn't the only one who missed it! You said left."

"Did I?" she said breezily.

Joe sighed and began to look for an exit to turn around.

They found their way onto Interstate 45…along with a million other people who probably had the same idea to catch a flight out of Houston. But at least they were moving. Joe checked the clock. It was almost three. If they could make it by six, they had a decent chance of getting out tonight, before the strike—

"I need a bathroom," Kate said.

"Oh my God," Joe muttered. "I thought you went at McDonald's."

"I did! I have a small bladder." She smiled sunnily, as if she were proud of it.

This was going to be the longest drive of his life, Joe thought. No contest. He took the next exit.

Chapter 4

WHEN KATE EMERGED FROM THE BATHROOM AT the Shell station, she felt sticky. It was overcast, warm, and very humid, which made it difficult to believe that a blizzard was engulfing half the country.

Joe was leaning against the front bumper. He'd removed his tie and stripped down to shirtsleeves, which he'd rolled up. His arms were crossed over his chest, and his biceps, Kate could not help noticing, were bulging against the fabric of his shirt. What did he do, spend every spare minute in a gym?

If a girl was going to be caught up in a catastrophe, it didn't hurt to be caught up with a guy as handsome as Joe…Somebody. Even if he did exhibit some Typical Male-ish tendencies from time to time.

But he looked good with his dark hair and blue eyes, and Kate, out of habit, smiled at him. Joe seemed surprised by her smile for some reason, and his gaze flicked over her face…lingering a moment too long on her mouth. "All better?" he asked.

"Much. Are you ready?"

"Baby, I was ready an hour ago," he said casually and pushed off the bumper of the rental car.

"I'm just going to move my bag first," Kate said as she walked to the passenger side of the car. "There's not enough room for me and this."

She reached down to the floorboard and attempted to lift the bag with two hands, but it was wedged in.

"Here, I'll get it."

She hadn't heard Joe come up behind her and abruptly straightened up and twisted about, knocking into him when she did. Yep. His body was as hard as a turtle shell, just like she'd guessed. She blinked up at him as he reached around her and lifted the bag out. He tossed it onto the floor behind the front passenger seat. "What is in that thing, anyway?" he asked as he walked around the back of the car to the driver's side.

"Work," she said, sliding into the passenger seat.

Joe started the car. "What kind of work?"

"I am an editor," Kate said proudly. "Well, assistant editor," she amended. "But on track to be a full editor."

"What, like books?"

No, like nursery rhymes. "Yes. Like books."

He glanced at her and smiled wryly. "You don't have to say it like I am one step above a cow on the food chain."

"I didn't say it like you were one step above a cow," she said pertly, although she was aware that she had.

"What kind of books?" he asked.

Kate sat a little straighter in her seat as he pulled out of the parking lot. "Women's fiction."

"Women's fiction," he repeated carefully. "Would that be fiction about women?"

"It's fiction about relationships. And love. That sort of thing."

Joe gave her a dubious look. "You mean romance novels," he said, as if he'd just figured out a complicated puzzle. "What do they call them? Bodice rippers." He laughed.

"First of all, they are not only romance, and secondly, that is so ignorant," Kate said. "It's a cliché, and you wouldn't say it if you actually bothered to read one."

"What makes you think I haven't read one?"

"*Have* you?" she demanded.

"No!" he said with a laugh as if that was ridiculous. "I don't *read*," he added. "I mean, tech manuals, yes. But not *books*." He laughed again as if the mere suggestion was ludicrous. "Especially not books about relationships. I'd rather watch sports."

"Do you know how primitive you sound right now?" Kate said.

"Why? Because I would rather watch sports than read about other people having sex?" He winked at her. "See, I don't need to read about it."

Kate rolled her eyes. "And what do *you* do, Mr. Never Cracked a Book?"

"Hey, I take issue with that," he said with playful bravado. "I've cracked a few books in my time. I'm in technology, which—and this may surprise you—actually requires a fairly high level of reading comprehension. I create security systems for banks."

"*Knew* it," Kate said pertly.

"Knew what?"

"That you were probably in something like technology."

"What's that mean?" he asked. "Why did you think that?"

He looked so genuinely surprised that Kate couldn't help but laugh. "Because you're like an IT guy. You know."

"No, I do *not* know," he said waspishly. "I do not fit the stereotype, and frankly, I don't know anyone in my field who does."

"So now you are offended by stereotypes?" Kate laughed. "That figures."

"What figures?"

"You don't like stereotypes. And I'm saying not all romance books fit the stereotype of bodice ripper, either."

Joe grinned. "Okay. Touché. I won't judge a bodice ripper by its cover until I read one. Who knows? It could happen."

Kate laughed. "No, it couldn't."

Joe grinned too—a warm, charming smile—and winked at her. "You're probably right. But I will reserve judgment just the same."

"Thank you," she said graciously.

"So tell me something, Kate. What is it about IT guys that get such a bad rap? I think we're kind of fun, actually."

Kate didn't get the chance to answer—her phone beeped. She picked it up and read the text message:

> Mom says air controller strike. Maybe good reason to call it off?

"What is the *matter* with her?" Kate demanded of no one, and dialed Lisa's number.

"I knew you'd call," Lisa said somberly.

"What the hell, Lisa?" Kate said sternly. "Why

are you suddenly so unsure of everything? Just two weeks ago you were telling me that Kiefer was the best thing that ever happened to you. Are you going to tell me that now, after four years, in the space of two weeks he has gone from perfect to you wanting to call it off?"

"No! Sort of," Lisa moaned. "I don't know, Kate—I just have this bad feeling that he doesn't really want to marry me."

"Why? Why why why?" Kate asked angrily.

"Okay, like the other day," Lisa said. "I was trying to get him to help me with the drink menu for the rehearsal dinner. I mean, it's *his* responsibility, but do you think he has taken charge? *Nooo*. So I said, okay, this has to get done, and I sat down with him, and I said, 'I'm going to help you, but we have to decide what we are serving. Do you like wine?' And he was like, 'I guess,' and I said, 'Okay, what about liquor? Are we serving liquor? Because I don't want everyone getting wasted before my wedding day, which means you, by the way—'"

"*Me?*" Kate exclaimed.

"No, no, not *you*. Kiefer. I said that to Kiefer, because you know how he is, Kate. You know. So anyway, he wouldn't make any decisions at all and he finally said, 'Why don't *you* do it, Lisa? You've made up your mind.' I mean, he was *totally* abdicating to me, like he has the whole way with this wedding. He wouldn't help me decide about the church, or the flowers, or how big or small the guest list was. He just tells me to do it and then goes off and watches basketball. What does that say to you? It says to me he doesn't really want to get married."

"Wow," Kate said. "Yes, I agree he could be just a little more supportive of you. After all, this is his wedding too," she said. "But it sounds to me like he's just being childish about it, and not that he doesn't want to marry you. If he didn't want to marry you, he's the kind of guy who would tell you, don't you think?" Kate looked to Joe for confirmation. He gave her an affirmative nod.

"I don't know," Lisa said.

"Well, I do. You're overreacting. Just relax. Pick the drinks for the rehearsal dinner. Tell Kiefer you guys need to talk about things—"

Joe suddenly shook his head, quite adamantly.

"But later. Much later," Kate added, and Joe nodded. "Right now, just focus on the wedding and how long you've been planning it, and how gorgeous you are going to be."

That seemed to appease Lisa. "You're right. It is going to be beautiful, isn't it? And I am going to be gorgeous. Did you just love the centerpieces? I can't wait to see you in that dress, Kate."

Kate rolled her eyes heavenward.

"Just be careful with it. That taffeta really wrinkles."

"I know," Kate said patiently.

"So when is your flight out?"

"Ah…" Kate quickly debated telling Lisa the truth. She rubbed the nape of her neck. "I'm not sure yet. They are rerouting a lot of people. But I'll let you know. So, listen, I have to run—"

"I just hope you get out before the air traffic controller strike, because that is the *last* thing I need to deal with," Lisa said. "I *cannot* be without my maid of honor. I'd just as soon reschedule."

Lord. "You won't have to do that," Kate said as confidently as she could manage. "Do you still have that spa package I gave you? Did you schedule that massage?"

"No. But that is a great idea," Lisa said absently. "Yeah, I think I'll do that."

"Great. So, listen, I better see about this flight. I'll call you later?"

She said good-bye and looked at Joe.

"See about what flight?"

"Trust me, it was the right thing to do," Kate said with a flick of her wrist. "Why are guys so damned insensitive?"

"Why are women so damned sensitive?" he easily countered. "What is it now?"

"Kiefer—that's my cousin's fiancé—is not helping," Kate said, and she related the story of Lisa and
Kiefer to Joe, from how long they'd been together,
to Kiefer's grand proposal with Christmas lights
and a high school chorus, to the last-minute wedding jitters and unwillingness to help.

Joe listened with a frown of concentration.
When she'd finished, he said, "Wow."

"I know, right?" Kate said. "He's really being
a jerk."

"I was thinking she was the jerk," Joe said.

Kate blinked. "*Lisa?* Lisa is doing everything!"

"And that's your problem right there," Joe said.
"She's so caught up in this wedding and it being
perfect that she isn't letting him do anything. He
doesn't have any ownership in it. It's like he's been
cut out."

"That's what I think—he's being childish."

"I didn't say that," Joe said. "I think he's just
being a guy."

"A guy," she repeated with a bit of derision in
her voice.

"Yes. A *guy*," he repeated firmly.

"So…you don't think he's having second
thoughts?"

"Nah," Joe scoffed. "First of all, he wouldn't
have asked her to marry him if he didn't love her.

Second, he is doing what he thinks he should be doing—giving her everything he thinks she wants. If he didn't want in, he would say so."

That almost made sense to Kate. "You sound like you've been down this path before."

"Me?" He laughed. "Hardly. But my brother has. Twice to be exact, and both women were totally eaten up with the wedding instead of the marriage."

Kate scarcely heard the last bit. She was focused on the *hardly*. "Why do you say it that way?" she asked him.

"Say what?"

"*Hardly*. You said hardly, like it was so out of the realm of possibility for you. Are you opposed to marriage?"

He gave her a bemused smile. "How on earth did you get that from what I just said? I'm not opposed to marriage. I don't think it's for me, but I'm not opposed to it."

"Why not?" she asked curiously. It was funny, but she'd had the same feeling about herself.

"I don't know," he said with a shrug. "I guess I've just never felt like I wanted to spend the rest of my waking days with one person."

"A guy like you?" she asked disbelievingly. She would think he'd have his pick of women.

"Who, an IT nerd?" he asked with a chuckle.

"No. A handsome man. A gentleman. I would think you had lots of girlfriends."

"Handsome, huh?" He grinned. "Yeah, I've had a few girlfriends along the way."

"But not one that you felt that way about."

"No," he said and looked at her curiously. "Why? Is that so strange?"

Something about that made Kate feel a little uncomfortable, but she wasn't certain why. "Maybe you're too busy partying," she said.

"What?" Joe laughed. "Where did that come from?"

"Because this morning, you smelled slightly of alcohol. And you looked really hungover."

Joe's eyes widened with surprise.

"Dark circles, your hair messed up—"

"Okay, okay," he said and laughed. "So maybe I had a few too many last night. But it's not what you think, kiddo. I happened to be the person of honor at a going-away party."

"Really?" she said, doubly curious now. "Why? Where are you going?"

"Seattle, remember?" He grinned at her. "I'm on my way to a new job. The kind of job that comes around once in a lifetime."

"Congratulations!" she said and ignored the tiny niggle of disappointment she felt.

"Thanks." He smiled happily. "So what about you?"

"I'm from Seattle. But now I live in New York."

"No, I mean the marriage thing. Have you ever gotten close?"

"Umm…no," she admitted. "Never."

"Okay. That's surprising too."

Kate could feel herself blushing. "Not really."

"Yes it is. You're very pretty," he said, and Kate felt the heat began to creep into her cheeks. "And you're smart. And, bonus points, you're a trouper."

"I am?" she asked, absurdly pleased by that compliment.

"So far," he said laughingly. "So why hasn't someone snatched you up?"

"Oh, come on—"

"No, really," he said. "I can't tell you how many women I meet who can't hang. Or maybe they can hang, but they can't *talk*." He shook his head. "It's disappointing, you know? You take a woman out to dinner, and she's hot, and then you discover she can't carry on an intelligent conversation."

"Are you kidding?" Kate asked. "What about being on the other side of the table? How many guys have I gone out with and then found out they are unread and uninterested in anything but sports scores?" She realized she'd just described what she knew of him and looked at him in horror.

But Joe laughed. "Touché, madam, touché. But you haven't answered the question. Why haven't you settled down?"

Kate smiled wryly. "I guess because I never felt that way about anyone, either. But unlike you, I didn't have a string of boyfriends to choose from."

"Now that's just too hard to believe," Joe said. "I'd think there'd be a line around the block, your poor navigation skills notwithstanding."

Kate laughed softly, but her cheeks were burning with self-consciousness. And pleasure. "At least I'm not an armrest hog," she said.

"Oh no, you're not going to pin that on me." Joe laughed. "*You* are *horrible* with the armrest."

"Everyone knows the middle seat gets the armrest!"

"I have never heard anything so ridiculous in my life," he scoffed. "You've got some wacky ideas floating behind those pretty green eyes, Kate."

She couldn't help it—she laughed.

"So how do you become an assistant editor?" he asked.

"You read a lot. And majoring in English helped. How do you become an IT guy?"

"You start by taking computers apart to see if you can put them back together."

Kate could picture a mop-top boy doing just that. "What is it about boys, always wanting to take things apart?"

"Sexist," he playfully accused her. "My sister is the one who showed me how. Why do girls always read a lot?"

"It's in our DNA. It so happens that there are more women book lovers than men."

"Include more sports scores and more men would read," he offered, smiling at Kate's laughter. "But the real question is, how do we get more women to deconstruct computers?"

"Good question," Kate said. "Computers are like cars. They should just work. No one wants to know how."

For the remainder of the drive to Houston, they argued playfully about the differences between men and women, and about who had the wherewithal to get to Seattle first.

As they entered the outskirts of Houston, rain began to fall. By the time they made their way across town to Houston's Intercontinental Airport, the rain had turned into a deluge. "You don't think this rain will delay flights even more, do you?" Kate asked, peering up at the sky as they dropped the rental car off.

"No, not at all," Joe said with a roll of his eyes. He grabbed Kate's bags.

"You don't have to do that," she said.

"I know," he said with a wink. "Come on, get that pink life raft and let's go find a flight out of here."

They crowded onto the shuttle, Kate with the garment bag on her back, Joe with her shoulder bag slung over his shoulder and cases in each hand. They ignored the looks of everyone who eyed her pink bag with disdain, then piled into the terminal with everyone else.

And into pandemonium.

"What the hell?" Joe said absently as they looked around.

A man standing just in front of them turned around. "The air traffic controllers just went on strike," he said.

Chapter 5

"WE HAVE TO GET THAT CAR BACK," KATE SAID instantly, crowding into Joe's side as a melee of angry, disgruntled passengers pushed and shoved toward the ticket counters. Joe couldn't help himself; he put a protective arm around Kate.

"We know what's going to happen," she said frantically. "Once they figure out they can't fly out, they will try and drive out, like us." She suddenly twisted into Joe's chest and grabbed his lapel, her green eyes wild. "We have to *go*."

"We can't drive out of this," Joe said, putting a hand on her arm. "It's at least a two-day drive in the best of weather, and we'd be driving into a blizzard."

Kate's grip tightened. "I think I am going to pass out."

"No, you're not," he evenly assured her, and gave her a comforting squeeze on the arm. "What about a train?"

"Train?"

"Yes, train," Joe said again and gently peeled free the fingers clawed around his lapel so he could reach his cell phone. "If we can just get farther west, we have more options for getting to Seattle." At least he hoped that was true. He googled the Amtrak schedules and squinted at the screen. "Okay, we can book a ticket right now, leaving in a couple of hours, and arriving in Phoenix at 6:30 tomorrow night."

"Tomorrow!" Kate exclaimed and did a dramatic little backward bend. "But that's the dress rehearsal! I'll miss the dress rehearsal, and I bought a gorgeous new dress to counter the peach thing!"

Joe looked up from his phone. "Do you know any other way to get there?"

Kate sighed with resignation. She looked down and shook her head. Tendrils of hair shook loose from the knot she'd tied in her hair earlier, and Joe had an insanely stupid urge to touch them, brush them back behind her ear.

"Listen, the important thing is that you get there in time for the wedding, right? And for me, Monday morning. I have to be there by Monday." He googled the location of the train station, then looked at Kate. "Should I buy the tickets?"

"*Yes*," she said and punched him lightly in the chest for emphasis.

As it turned out, getting the tickets was the easy part. Getting across town looked impossible. The taxi stands were swimming with humans trying to leave the airport.

After twenty minutes of waiting, Joe was getting a little panicky himself. He'd been to Houston only a couple of times, but what he remembered was that it was huge and sprawling. He imagined that sprawl would seem to double in a rainstorm. "If we can't get in a cab soon, we won't make it," he said grimly.

"We're going to make it," Kate said, her determination returned.

"I don't think so," Joe said, looking at his watch.

"Okay, that's it," Kate said and thrust the pink garment bag at him. "Hold this for me, please."

"Wait—where are you going?" he called after her, but Kate was marching up the line, her hips moving enticingly in the pencil skirt she was wearing. As her fair head disappeared into the crowd of people, he lost sight of her altogether.

Several minutes passed. Joe kept looking at his watch, wondering if he should go after her or stay put. When he looked up from his watch for what seemed like the hundredth time, he saw her walking back. But she was not alone—a porter with a red cart was walking alongside her.

And Kate was crying.

Joe's pulse instantly leaped. "Kate!" he shouted. His instinct was to go to her, but he had a stronger instinct to keep their place in line. "Kate, what's wrong?" he demanded as she walked up to him, her face streaked with the path of her tears. It alarmed him so that he grabbed her arms. "What happened? Are you all right?"

"Joe, it's *Dad*," she exclaimed, sniffling up at him as the porter stood uncomfortably to the side. "He's taken a turn for the worse. I got the call when I went to check on how long it would be."

"What?" Joe asked, confused. "Your dad?"

She suddenly grabbed his upper arms and squeezed so tight it was almost painful. "Joe," she said, her eyes narrowing just slightly. "I know you thought we'd make it on time, but unless we make that train, I won't see him again!" She burst into tears and buried her face in Joe's chest.

"Oh, the poor thing," a woman behind him said.

"Oh my God," Joe said. He was fairly certain there was no father issue and that Kate was working some mysterious, probably nonsensical angle, but then again, he didn't really know her. He couldn't be sure. He put his hand on the back of Kate's head, held her close to him. "I'm so *sorry*."

"Don't worry—one of our private car passengers

is going to give you a ride," the porter said and gestured at Kate. "So she doesn't have to wait for a cab," he added in a loud whisper. "Are these your bags here?"

"What?"

Kate groaned and squeezed his arms again. Quite tightly. And then she grasped a bit of his coat fabric and gave it a tug. Wow. She'd found them a *ride*? He would take back every thought he'd just had about this being nonsense.

"Young man, he is asking if these are your bags," the kindly woman said behind him.

"Oh. Yes. Those," Joe said.

"Listen, you need to pull yourself together and help her," the woman continued and patted his back. "She needs to say good-bye to her father. Now go take advantage of the offer and get to the train station before it's too late."

"Right," Joe said. "Thank you." To the porter he said, "Don't forget the pink thing." He put his arm around Kate's shoulders and pulled her tightly into his side. "Be strong, baby," he said. "We have to be strong for Dad." What was that he saw, the barest hint of a smile?

"I just need him to hang on a little longer," she said tearfully. "Why now?" she sobbed as they followed the porter to a black town car. "It's so unfair!"

Joe squeezed her tight in a silent plea not to overdo it.

In the backseat of the town car sat a woman in an expensive suit with a Louis Vuitton briefcase at her feet. She smiled sympathetically at Joe. "I'm so sorry," she said softly to Joe as he climbed in behind a limp Kate. "She is obviously very close to her father."

"So close," Joe said.

"It's so unexpected," Kate said through her tears.

"Right," Joe said, smiling ruefully at their benefactor as he tucked Kate into his body. "We can't thank you enough for the ride—she's a basket case."

Kate poked him in the side.

"I'm just so glad I can help." The woman leaned forward a bit to look at Kate, whose hair, thankfully, covered her face. Kate shuddered and made a sort of garbled sobbing noise. The woman eased back, glanced over Kate's head, and gave Joe a look brimming with sympathy.

As the car started slipping into traffic, Joe very slyly gave Kate a slight fist bump.

By the time they reached the train station, Kate had feigned a slight recovery. She was still tucked into Joe's side, which, he had to admit, he liked. She felt good next to him. All warm and soft. She was speaking somberly to the woman beside her, telling her what a great dad her father was. "Of all the times this would happen." She sighed. "The blizzard, the strike…"

"It's horrible," the woman agreed. "It took me two days to come home from London due to all the cancellations. I'm just glad I don't have to go any farther." The car coasted to a stop in front of the train station. "I wish you both the best of luck," she said. "Take care of yourself, Kate."

"Thank you. I will." Kate teared up again, and she took the woman's hands in both of hers. "Thank you so much."

Joe said his thanks, too, but hopped out as soon as he could and raced the driver to the trunk. The less pink the Good Samaritan saw, the better. He didn't want to her to be reminded of a wedding and start putting two and two together. He watched Kate come out of the town car, watched her bend over and wave, then stand there as the town car pulled away.

"Well played," Joe said. "Where did you learn to *cry* like that?"

"Drama club, Garfield High," Kate said morosely, then twirled around, arms wide. "God, what have I done, Joe? I just *lied* to that poor woman to get to the front of the line! What has *happened* to me? I don't lie to get my way! But look, the first sign of adversity and I am lying and crying and becoming someone I don't even recognize!"

"It's called survival," Joe said.

"I never felt so greasy in all my life," she said, running her palms down her thighs. "I'm a horrible person."

"Take it easy, Kate," Joe said and unthinkingly smoothed her hair back from her brow. "Ask yourself this: Would you rather lie to a complete stranger? Or call Lisa and tell her you can't make her wedding?"

Big green eyes blinked up at him and something shiny flashed in them. Kate grabbed her shoulder bag. "Come on, we have a train to catch." She swung her bag over her shoulder, hoisted the garment bag onto her back, and stalked toward the entrance.

You had to admire a woman like that, Joe thought. And he did. More than he would have ever expected upon first seeing her. Definitely way more than he wanted to.

—⁂—

It should not have come as a surprise that squeezing onto the overcrowded train was a bit like squeezing into the proverbial sardine can. Joe and

Kate scarcely made it on time, and as it took longer than normal to maneuver the pink raft through the cars, they could not find seats together. Joe sat two rows back from Kate. All he could see of her was the edge of the pink garment bag that she held on her lap. The bottom of it stuck out into the aisle, and he winced every time someone walked by and stepped on it.

Joe dozed on and off as the train trundled along, rocking gently side to side. Somewhere in the night he was rudely awakened by the harsh whisper of his name. When he opened his eyes, he saw only pink plastic, and then felt the pressure of a knobby knee on his thigh.

"Ouch!" he said as Kate half crawled, half fell over him into the seat next to him. He had no idea what had happened to the young woman sitting beside him. He had not seen her or felt her move over him to leave.

Kate landed with a thud.

"What time is it?" Joe asked with a yawn.

"Two," Kate said and dragged the garment bag across their bodies, stuffing it into the space between her and the window. Apparently, she'd given up on trying to keep the dress wrinkle-free. She dug in her shoulder bag and handed him a prewrapped sandwich.

"What's this?"

"Supper," she said. "I got them from the dining car before they closed. I hope you like tuna."

Joe did like tuna—from his kitchen. He was entirely suspicious of a prewrapped tuna sandwich from an Amtrak dining car. But then again, he was starving, and desperate times called for desperate measures.

Kate reached in her bag again and produced two cans of iced tea—another cause for gag reflex—and the pièce de résistance, a carefully wrapped chocolate-chip cookie that was the size of a small dinner plate. "Last one," she said proudly and placed it on her lap, then unwrapped her tuna sandwich.

They both took a bite, chewing carefully. "May I ask you something?" she asked before taking another bite of a sandwich that looked just as soggy as his.

"Sure," Joe said.

"Do you believe in fate?"

Joe almost choked on the tuna. Generally, when a woman asked him if he believed in fate, it was the lead-in to a conversation about feelings. Joe did not like to talk about feelings. Most of the time he didn't even like to acknowledge he had them. Feelings, especially where women were concerned, were never clear-cut for him. They were messy and sticky, and he never seemed to say or feel the right thing.

He looked at Kate, who was making nice work of a disgusting tuna sandwich. She didn't really strike him as the kind of woman who wanted to discuss feelings, either. "Why do you ask? Do you?" he asked.

"I don't know," she said and glanced at the window. There was nothing but black out there—they were passing through desert. "Most of the time, I'd say no. But today has been kind of weird. It almost feels like this was supposed to happen."

"What was supposed to happen?" he asked carefully.

"Me having such a difficult time getting to Seattle," she said, and Joe felt a rush of relief. "I mean, Lisa is teetering on the edge, and I am the only one who can get through to her. So I have to wonder, all these obstacles…" She looked at Joe and shrugged. "If, for some stupid reason, Lisa canceled the wedding, it's possible it's fate, right?"

Joe didn't know Lisa, but having listened in on two conversations, he figured it was more likely that Lisa was just a nut. "I think it would be more of a coincidence."

"Don't look at me like that," Kate said with a wry smile. "I may sound like a loon, but I'm not really. I've just been sitting on a train for the last few hours with nothing to do but think."

"I wasn't thinking you were crazy, Kate. I was just looking at you." He liked looking at her. She had some really expressive eyes, and he liked the way her nose was slightly upturned. And her mouth—hell, her *mouth*.

Joe made himself look at his sandwich. He wanted to kiss her. Just…*kiss* her.

"So, do you?" she asked.

"Pardon?" he asked with a small cough.

"Believe in fate."

"Ah…" He risked a look at her again. "Depends," he said noncommittally.

"Right," she said, nodding as if they'd just exchanged some meaningful ideas. "For me too."

But Joe was thinking only about sex at the moment, imagining that mouth and those eyes beneath him. He looked away to give himself a good and silent talking-to. Thinking about sex wasn't going to help anything. It wasn't going to get them to Seattle, and it would only complicate this fragile, weird alliance they'd formed.

But he couldn't stop thinking about it at two in the morning on a train crossing the desert.

"I'm so *tired*," Kate said and put down what was left of her sandwich. She leaned back and closed her eyes. "You can have the cookie," she said through a yawn.

Joe smiled. He gazed at her, wondering how he could have missed just how pretty she was when she knocked into him this morning in New York with the pink raft. Was that really just this morning? He felt as if he'd known her a lot longer than that.

He silently admired her features, right up to the moment her head slid down on his shoulder and she began to snore.

Chapter 6

LISA TOOK THE NEWS ABOUT KATE'S DELAY WITH a lot of whining, wailing, and "How am I going to *do* this without you?"

Kate talked her neurotic cousin off the ledge. She made her understand that she was only missing a dinner, not a major event. It was one meal. Not a huge loss—besides the dress, it was not even a small loss. Lisa said she understood. She even seemed to agree with Kate.

But not fifteen minutes after Kate had hung up, her mother called.

"When are you going to be here?" her mother demanded with a slightly accusatory tone.

"Mom, seriously. I am on a *train* to Phoenix. A train! I started on a plane, then a car, and now I am on a TRAIN. I am doing the best I can."

"Well, I didn't say you weren't," her mother sniffed. "It just seems like you could have rented a car or something."

"Mom, do you know where Texas is? It is very far away from Seattle. You can't drive from Texas to Washington in a blizzard!"

She must have been speaking with agitation, because Joe put his broad hand on her knee and squeezed reassuringly.

"Oh, I know," her mother said wearily. "I was just hoping. We'll all be sick if you miss the wedding, and Lisa doesn't need any distractions. I've always said that girl is too high strung for her own good."

"I won't miss the wedding," Kate said firmly. "We are almost to Phoenix, and we hear they are bringing scabs in."

"Bringing *what*?"

"Scabs."

"Strikebreakers," Joe offered. He had removed his coat again and loosened his collar. His hair, thick and dark brown, looked as if he'd dragged his fingers through it a dozen times. And he had a very sexy shadow of a beard that Kate had to tell herself not to stare at.

"Who is that?" her mother demanded, jarring Kate back to the present.

"Ah… Joe."

"Joe! Who's Joe?"

"He was on my flight. We're both trying to get to Seattle."

"Oh. You should invite him to the wedding," her mother said cheerfully, as if Kate and Joe were sitting in a café sipping mimosas. She'd never heard of Joe until this moment and was inviting him to a major family event. Her family was crazy.

"Oh my God," her mother said suddenly. "Here comes your aunt. I wonder what the crisis is *now*," she muttered irritably. "You'd think Lisa was the first woman to ever get married. Katie, sweetheart, keep us posted. We'll hold the wedding for you if necessary!"

"Mom, you can't hold the wedding," Kate said, but her mother had already signed off.

Kate clicked off, made a sound of severe frustration, and Joe laughed.

"Your family sounds as crazy as mine."

"I think I've got you beat," Kate said. "Where is your family, anyway?"

"Scattered," he said. "My brother is in Paris—"

"Paris!"

"Married to a Frenchwoman. My dad and sister are in Connecticut and my mom in Illinois. Yours?"

"All in Seattle," Kate said. "My aunt and uncle—Lisa's parents—live right around the corner. It's like some weird religious-sect compound, everyone always back and forth." Joe laughed, but he had no idea how tied up in each other's business they all were.

"So while you were assuring your mother you're not just playing hooky, I was digging for news. It looks as if the major airports, like Phoenix, will have enough controllers to get a few flights off the ground."

Kate gasped. "Really? You mean we might really get to Seattle?"

"If we can book a flight," he said. "I'm going to make a call. I've got a kick-ass travel agent."

He punched in the number and then said, "Hey, Brenda. It's Joe." And he smiled. It was a very easy, very sexy smile, and Kate imagined it could melt the false eyelashes off a woman. "Remember that trip we booked to Seattle? Well, I've run into a little trouble…"

Fifteen minutes later, Kate sat with her arms folded tightly across her, mildly annoyed at the number of times Joe chuckled. If he was going to book a flight, she didn't see why he didn't just *book* it instead of chatting on and on with Brenda, whoever she was, who was probably old enough to be his mother.

"Okay, we'll book Kate onto that flight," he said. "Hold on." He covered his phone. "What's your last name, anyway?"

"Preston."

"Preston," he said into the phone. "Just put it on my account. And yeah, I'll take the next one."

"What next one? You're not flying with me?" Kate asked.

Joe grabbed her hand and wrapped his fingers around hers, holding it against his rock-hard thigh. "Great. Thanks, Brenda. I owe you those Maroon 5 tickets."

Rats. Maroon 5 was not a grandma band.

Joe clicked off and beamed at Kate, squeezing her hand. "You're booked on the last seat of that flight tonight, Kate Preston."

She gasped. "Are you kidding?"

"Would I kid about something like that? Yes, for real."

"What about you?"

"I'm going tomorrow. But I don't have to be there until Monday. You needed to be there yesterday."

He was smiling. He was happy to have arranged it. Kate made herself smile. "Thank you. I owe you. Again."

"Not to worry," he said. He looked at her strangely. "What's the matter? I thought you'd be happy."

"I *am*," she said, nodding adamantly. "I just…" *Really like you. Sorta don't want this to end. Want to write a sitcom about two people who meet on a plane…*

Kate looked away from his silvery blue eyes.

"You know what? I don't think that tuna-fish sand-wich was a good idea."

He laughed. "It was a *horrible* idea. I'm going to book a hotel room. After that, I'll take you on in Words with Friends if you're up to it."

Kate jerked her gaze to him. "Oh, I'm up to it," she said, digging out her phone. "I am *so* up to it."

—⁓—

The hours, she was sad to note, flew by as they played Words with Friends until Joe lost juice in his phone. By that time, they were nearing the Phoenix station, slightly ahead of schedule. Joe had taken care of everything, including transport to the airport, and refused all of her efforts to repay him.

They arrived at the airport in a transport van—Joe, Kate, their bags, and a crumpled pink garment bag. Kate didn't have the heart to look at the bridesmaid dress now. She could see that one side of it wasn't as poufy as it had been starting out and shuddered to think what else had happened in there.

Joe got out with her, helped her with her bags. "So," he said, shoving his hands through his hair. "I guess this is it."

"I guess so," Kate said. She tried to smile. "I don't know your last name," she said.

"Firretti," he said.

"Firretti," she repeated, savoring the name a moment. "It sounds so…"

"Intelligent?" he offered.

Kate laughed. "I was going to say sporty."

Joe smiled.

"So…you're moving to Seattle."

"I am. And you're staying in New York."

"Yeah," she said softly.

Joe touched her cheek with his knuckle. "I have to say, although you suck at navigating, I can't imagine a better partner in this little jaunt across the country."

That made Kate feel warm and tingly all over. "And I should say that although you're a terrible armrest hog, I'm really glad you ended up next to me."

Joe stroked her cheek, touched her earlobe, then reluctantly dropped his hand. "Take care, Kate. Call me if you need anything."

"Okay…but your phone is dead."

"Right. I'm going to charge it at the airport Hilton," he said, jerking his thumb over his shoulder. "In about thirty minutes, it will be good to go. So, call me if something comes up."

"Okay," she said weakly. "You should call me too. I can give you some tips about Seattle if you need them."

"I'll do that," he promised.

There was nothing left to say. Kate smiled ruefully.

Joe sighed, took her elbow in hand, and leaned forward to kiss her cheek. "Take care, Kate. But go now, or you'll miss your flight." He picked up her bag and put it on her shoulder.

"Thanks," she said. "Seriously, Joe Firretti, thanks for everything." She picked up the garment bag, pulled the stem of her suitcase. "Bye."

"Good-bye, Kate."

Kate started walking, moving through the glass doors into cool, slightly fetid air. When the doors closed behind her, she glanced back.

Joe was still standing there, watching her. He lifted his hand.

So did Kate. She smiled again, then turned away, walking on, feeling exhausted, a little queasy, and indescribably sad.

Chapter 7

THE AIRPORT HOTEL WAS A LITTLE DINGY, THE room furnishings a little worn, but the only thing Joe cared about was that it had a shower and a bed. After he'd washed the last thirty-six hours from his body, he pulled on some lounge pants and ordered a burger, fries, and a beer, and settled in to catch up on sports.

But his gaze kept shifting to the window, from which he would see the occasional planes the scabs managed to send out over the red mountains of Phoenix.

Joe was not particularly proud of it, but a few years ago, he had been a real dog when it came to women. That was how he'd met Brenda the Travel Agent. She was nice, but turned out to be a little vanilla for his tastes.

Fortunately, their short dating history had ended well, and the girl could work some travel magic.

He knew because part of his job had been to travel, and Brenda had always managed to get him home without much trouble. Uprisings, tsunamis, volcano ash, and terrorist threats were no match for her.

Joe was glad she'd gotten Kate into the last seat on the last flight out to Seattle. Glad in a non-doglike, adult way of doing something nice for someone for a change. So why was he hoping Kate hadn't made that plane? And what sort of dumbass was he for not asking to see her in Seattle? He'd thought about it—of course he had—but that thought had been followed by a bunch of other thoughts crowding in and stifling it, like *Why*, and *What's the point*, and *Get a grip, it's just a girl.*

Yeah. A girl. A really cool, really good-looking girl. A girl who had somehow managed to make him sit up and take notice like he hadn't done in a very long time.

Smooth, Firretti.

The sun was beginning to set, and Joe couldn't see the planes anymore. Kate had obviously made it—her flight would have departed a half hour ago, and she hadn't called. He closed his eyes and listened to the ESPN guy talk about the Phoenix Suns' chances this season.

A knock on the door brought him off the bed. "Thank God," he said. His stomach was growling.

He walked to the door and opened it, then stumbled back a step with surprise.

"I hope you don't mind," Kate said apologetically from just behind the pink raft.

"No," Joe said quickly. "You missed your flight?"

"Ah…rescheduled. First thing tomorrow." Kate winced and put a hand to her belly. "I wasn't feeling too well. Tuna fish, I think."

His grin was slow but broad. "That was some rank tuna fish," he agreed. "You'd better come in."

She smiled and pushed the pink raft at him. "Thanks!"

He wrestled the garment bag into the rack behind him, and when he turned back, Kate held up a six-pack of beer. "I thought beer would help my tummy," she said. "And you seem like a beer guy."

"I'm going to take that as a compliment," he said, grabbing her bags and pulling them in. "Where did you get that, anyway?"

"From the same guy who told me what room you're in," she said. "I have my ways."

"Don't tell me. I might be jealous." He grinned at her and stepped back to allow her entry. "By the way, just what does a beer guy look like?" he asked as she slipped past him.

Kate paused. Her gaze dropped to his bare chest,

to his lounge pants, and slowly rose again. "Like *that*," she said. Her voice had changed. "Just like that," she added quietly.

Joe could feel the draw between them, the unmistakable chemistry kicking up and swirling about them into a lethal mix of desire and admiration. It felt as if everything Joe had ever wanted in a woman was standing right in front of him—with too many clothes on, but still—and he was vaguely amazed he'd ever let her walk into that airport without him. He wanted to say all those things, but he felt strangely tongue-tied. He could only reach for her, and at the same moment, she leaped at him.

Joe crushed her to him, his mouth on her lips, as soft and lush as he'd imagined them to be. Kate grabbed his head between her hands and teased him with her tongue, plunging him into a familiar fog of arousal and desire. But this was different than the usual. This felt deeper and somehow more important.

He whirled her around and pushed her up against the door. Her warm, wet mouth was as tormenting to him as it was pleasurable. Her body curved into his, rattling him in every bone, in every nerve. He thrust his hands into her hair, moved his mouth to her neck.

He'd never felt anything as strongly as he was

feeling the need to be with Kate—beside her, around her, in her. He caressed her sides, her torso, her breasts, and Kate made a little groaning sigh into his mouth that sent him careening down a slope of yearning.

He whirled her around again, crashing into the rack that passed as a closet.

"Not the dress!" she whispered frantically against his cheek, and Joe whirled again, bumping into the mirror tacked to the wall. The thing came off and crashed behind Kate.

Joe suddenly threw his arms around her waist and lifted her up off her feet, falling onto the bed with her. He dipped down to the hollow of her throat, to the vee in her shirt, tasting her skin, feeling the faint beat of her heart, racing in time with his.

A pounding at the door made them both freeze. Kate stared wide-eyed at him.

"Burger," he muttered to her deliciously creamy breasts.

Kate gasped. "*Burger*," she repeated lustfully, and abruptly pushed him off her. She jumped up, buttoning her blouse as she hurried to the door. Joe groaned and fell face forward onto the bed. He heard her thanking whoever had brought it, assuring that person she had the tray under control. The door shut, and a moment later, Kate reappeared with the room service tray, her hair charmingly messed, her blouse only crookedly rebuttoned, and a french fry sticking out of the side of her mouth. She slid the tray onto the desk.

Joe grabbed her around the waist and pulled her back down onto the bed. "But I'm *starving*," Kate laughingly implored him.

"So am I," he growled and began to kiss her neck as he unbuttoned her blouse again.

She sighed softly. Her hands were moving on him again, sweeping over his arms and hips. She dropped her head back with a gasp of pleasure as Joe sought more of her bare skin with his mouth. He felt like he had a rattlesnake under his skin, his body one mess of quivering, jangled nerves.

Kate pressed against the hard ridge of his erection and inhaled a ragged, ravenous breath. White-hot shivers of anticipation ran up Joe's spine. He rolled over, pulling her to straddle his lap. Kate cupped his face. Her gaze moved over his eyes, his nose, and his mouth. "Joe Firretti," she said softly, "where the hell did you come from?"

"I was wondering the same thing about you," he said, and pushed a golden lock back from her face. He kissed her softly, slid his hands to her shoulders, then her rib cage, and down, to her hips. He dipped a hand beneath the hem of her skirt and slid it up her thigh.

Kate's sigh was long and sweet. It reminded Joe of contentment, the sort of sound one might make when returning home, to the place they were meant to be. Her arms encircled his neck, and she kissed him back, slowly now, savoring it.

Joe found the zipper in her skirt and pulled it down, and somehow, between the two of them, she shimmied out of it. Her blouse had come completely undone, and underneath it she wore a lacy red bra that made his blood boil. He rolled again, putting Kate on her back, and moved his hand higher, touching the soft flesh of her inner thigh.

When his fingers brushed the apex of her legs, Kate reached for his lounge pants, her fingers finding the tie and undoing it, then pushing them down his hips, wrapping her fingers around him. Joe stroked her and Kate moved against his hand. She made a small cry of pleasure and Joe couldn't tolerate it another moment. He slid into her.

He began to move inside her, teetering on the edge of his own powerful climax, moving faster as Kate moved with him, her breath coming quicker and harder. Her fingers curled into his arms, and she suddenly lifted up, gasping with the sensation of her climax.

Joe couldn't contain himself; he flew apart and rained down in tiny bits of himself onto that bed.

Moments passed—blissful, satiated moments—before Kate cupped his face and smiled.

He smiled, too, could feel the satisfaction of that smile reaching deep into him. He gathered her in his arms and kissed her cheek, her hair, and her mouth once more before settling down with her tucked into his side. He could feel her lips curve into a smile against his chest, her fingers tracing a long and lazy line down his side.

"I am so glad you missed your flight," he said, still a little breathless.

"Me too," she agreed and giggled.

Chapter 8

SITTING ON THE BED, NUDE BUT FOR THE SHEET wrapped loosely about her, eating half of a man's burger and washing it down with his beer was the best post-coital experience Kate had ever had in her life.

She couldn't stop grinning. She'd never had sex like *that*, and it was a revelation to her. So many thoughts and feelings were fighting for recognition in her, bits and pieces of them scattering about in euphoria.

This, Kate thought, was what she wanted. This, right here, with this guy, Joe Firretti.

She grinned at him again. Joe didn't notice—he was too engrossed in the manuscript she was editing. He was propped up against a stack of pillows, the sheet covering him from the waist down. His brow was furrowed in concentration. Kate slipped her hand across his rock-hard abdomen, but Joe caught her wrist and squeezed lightly. "Stop that, you vixen," he said without looking up from the pages. "I have never used the word 'vixen' in my life until this moment. But I have to find out if she's going to let him in her house or not."

"Of course she does."

"Hey!" Joe protested, putting down the pages and casting a playfully stern frown at her. "Don't *tell* me. That ruins it."

Kate laughed. "If she doesn't let him in, there's no love story."

"Oh. I get it." He grinned and tossed the pages to the foot of the bed. "You're an expert, I take it," he said as he gathered her up in his arms. He kissed her, then snagged another fry. "Tell me what you like," he said.

"What I *like?*"

"Yes." He ate another fry. "What makes you happy? Puppies and ribbons? Rugby and scuba diving?"

Kate thought about that. "Shoes," she said with a definitive nod.

"I should have guessed that based on the weight of your suitcase alone. What else?"

This was what Kate was discovering she particularly liked about Joe. Yes, the sex was amazing, but better still, he was willing to talk. About everything. She tried to remember the last time she'd lounged on a bed—naked—and talked about sports and books and popular TV shows. She wondered if she'd ever known someone who would laugh with her about politics, or know the best sushi places in New York, or *agree* with her that Justin Bieber actually had put out a few catchy tunes.

Kate was not one for clichés. In the books she edited, she weeded them out and struck them from the pages. But at present she was wallowing in a cliché, because she truly, deeply felt as if she'd been waiting all her life for a guy like Joe Firretti to come around.

It sucked, it totally sucked that he was moving to Seattle. Fate—if such a thing existed—was playing the cruelest joke imaginable on her.

They watched Jimmy Kimmel, then took a shower together and made love again. Only slower. They took their time, learning each other, trying different things. And then they lay in the dark, Kate's head on his shoulder, their fingers laced together.

"Hey," Kate said. "Want to come to a wedding with me?"

Joe stroked her hair. "Do you promise to wear the mysterious pink-raft dress?"

She smiled in the dark. "If I haven't destroyed it."

"Then yes," Joe said and kissed the top of her head. "I would like to go to a wedding with you."

"Assuming we make it," Kate said.

"Oh, we'll make it, baby," Joe said. "We haven't even touched the boat industry yet."

Kate laughed. "We really did have quite an adventure, didn't we?"

"That's an understatement."

"So…do you believe in fate yet?" she teased him.

She could hear Joe's soft chuckle. "You have to admit, it's wild that we met like we did and ended up here, just to say good-bye in a day or so."

"'Wild' is not the word that comes to my mind."

Hers either, really. She could see his blue eyes in the light from the window, shining into hers. "We make a good team, Joe Firretti."

"We make an *excellent* team," he agreed. "Minus the navigation."

"And the armrest issue," she reminded him.

He grinned.

"If you were still in New York, do you think we'd… I mean, would it be presumptuous to think that maybe—"

"Baby," he said, "we'd *definitely* be checking out some sushi bars and the Giants games, are you kidding?"

She smiled, kissed his chest. That made her a little sad, really. "When you come to visit, we can do that, right?"

"Right. And when you're in Seattle," he added.

Right. She didn't let the thought that she only made it to Seattle twice this year—this being the second time—linger. Maybe she'd come back more often. Maybe she'd make editor and get a raise and come back at least once a month. She refused to allow the reality of her situation to ruin the moment.

Maybe Joe was hearing the tinny voice of reality, too, because neither of them spoke after that.

Kate couldn't say when she drifted off to sleep, but she was awakened by an alarm that brought her off the bed. She pushed her hair from her eyes and looked around. Joe was standing at the foot of the bed, grinning at her. He had on a pair of jeans, a white collared shirt, and a blue blazer. "Rise and shine, kid. We don't want to miss that plane. Weather says a big storm is headed for Pacific coast."

As much as Kate wanted to extend her stay with Joe, the thought of being stuck in Phoenix did not appeal. She dug a pair of yoga pants from her bag, as well as a tank top and hoodie.

Against all odds, when Joe and Kate arrived at the airport, the pink raft in tow, their flight to Seattle showed an on-time departure. At the gate, Kate stood at the window, staring at the plane that had somehow managed to fly in from Los Angeles, and called Lisa, waking her to tell her she'd make it to the wedding.

"Oh thank God!" Lisa said with relief. "Mom!" she shouted. "MOM! Kate's going to make it!"

"So is everything okay?" Kate asked as Joe appeared, two lattes in hand.

"Yes," Lisa said. "Why? What do you mean? Do you mean something?"

"No! But yesterday you were a little freaked out—"

"Pre-wedding jitters," Lisa said dismissively. Kate could hear her moving around, could hear water running. "Everyone says that's all it is."

Joe handed Kate a latte. She smiled at him. "So you're okay?" she asked again.

"Yes, I am okay," Lisa said, sounding like her normal self. "I mean, sure, Kiefer could have been slightly more supportive and all that, but I know that a guy like him only comes around once in a lifetime."

Kate lifted her gaze to Joe. He winked at her. "Tell me about it," she said. "By the way, I'm bringing someone to the wedding."

"Who?"

"The guy on my flight who helped me get across the country," Kate said. "His name is Joe Firretti."

"Yeah, bring him, bring him!" Lisa said excitedly. "Do you know that everything is shut down from Colorado east? It's a miracle you got as far as you did. We want to hug him!"

"No, please—"

"When are you getting in?"

"Ten this morning," Kate said.

She made arrangements with Lisa for someone to pick her up, then hung up and smiled a little tentatively at Joe. "They can't wait to meet you," she said.

"I can't wait to meet them," he said.

Yes, well, he might change his mind after the full force of the Prestons had been visited upon him.

Chapter 9

THEY WERE LUCKY TO BE ON THE SAME FLIGHT, Joe figured, even if they couldn't sit together. He could see just the top of Kate's head above a middle seat a few rows ahead of him and wondered if she'd begun her attack on the armrest yet. Every once in a while, she would sit up, turn around, and smile at him. She had happy eyes, he thought. Big, green, happy eyes. He wouldn't mind starting every day with big, green, happy eyes.

It seemed ridiculously unfair that Joe would meet a girl like Kate just as he was about to take the biggest step in his career. If he believed in fate, he would be calling it a few choice names right now.

They landed without a hitch in Seattle, but Joe could hear the guy behind him on the phone as they taxied to the gate. He was irate that the next leg of his flight had been canceled. Weather or air traffic, Joe didn't know. He was thankful he was at last where he needed to be. Disaster had been averted; he would meet the boss from Switzerland and begin his new job.

He didn't feel quite as excited about it as he had forty-eight hours ago.

Kate was waiting for him in the passenger ramp, the pink raft propped up beside her. She smiled brightly at him when she saw him and caught his hand. "Wait," she said as he tried to move forward, and pulled him to the side.

"What's wrong?"

"Okay," she said. "Listen. My family is tight. *Really* tight. So tight they can be a little overbearing," she said with a charming wince. "And I don't bring guys home a lot. Maybe never. So..." She shrugged.

Joe smiled at her angst. "Kate, it's okay," he said. "I can handle them." He picked up her garment bag, tossed it over his shoulder, and took her hand in his.

"So here we go," Kate said, looking down at their clasped hands as they made their way up the passenger ramp.

"Here we go, two people who have been brought together by an epic travel meltdown."

Kate smiled. But her smile didn't seem quite as bright as it had earlier this morning, when she'd been so deliciously naked in his bed. Families had a way of doing that to a person.

At the baggage claim area, the little scream of happiness Joe heard turned out to be for Kate. He turned just in time to see an older woman who looked like Kate barreling right toward them, a couple of guys and another woman with her.

"Oh thank God, you *made* it!" the woman shouted and threw her arms around Kate, squeezing her tightly, weaving back and forth. Then she suddenly put Kate at arm's length. "Where's the *dress*?"

"Right there," Kate said, pointing at Joe. Joe wondered how anyone in Seattle could have missed the arrival of the dress. "Mom," Kate said, "this is Joe Firretti."

"And the dress," Joe added, holding up the pink raft.

"Oh, thank God again," the woman said, her shoulders dropping with relief.

"This is my mom, Sandra," Kate said. "And my dad, James. And my brother Colton and my sister Cassidy."

"With a C," the young woman said.

"Pleasure," he said to them all, and he was still smiling when Kate's mother moved. Joe thought she meant to take the dress from him. But instead,

she threw her arms around him. "Thank you
so much for bringing my baby home," she said,
sounding almost tearful.

"He didn't bring me home," Kate said. "We
were on the same flight, and we were both coming
to Seattle."

"Don't try and downplay it, Katie-Kate," her
mother said, beaming up at Joe. "We owe this
young man a debt of gratitude."

"We'll pay him later, Sandra," Mr. Preston said,
and clapped Joe on the shoulder as if they were
old friends. "You didn't take any liberties with my
little girl, did you, son?"

"Dad!" Kate cried, clearly mortified.

Mr. Preston squeezed Joe's shoulder and
laughed. "Kidding! Come on, let's go. I told Glen
I'd help him get the bar set up."

"And we have hair and makeup this afternoon,"
Mrs. Preston added. "Come on, Joe, we've made
up a cot for you in the library."

"That's not necessary," he said quickly, holding
up a hand. "I've got a reservation—"

"Nonsense!" Mrs. Preston said firmly. "You
will come with us. We have plenty of room, and
after what you did for Kate, I wouldn't have it any
other way. Just call the hotel and tell them you'll
be there tomorrow."

"What makes you think he did it all?" Kate asked. "It's not like we mushed across the country."

"Don't be a sourpuss," Mr. Preston said cheerfully and grabbed her tote bag, handing it to Colton.

Kate looked helplessly at Joe. "See?"

He winked at her. He liked the Prestons. He liked them a lot.

The Prestons lived in the Queen Anne district of Seattle, an area of old and well-loved homes. The Preston house was a rambling turn-of-the-century, five-bedroom, three-bath home with wood floors and dark window casings and a view of Lake Union. It was charming and a little quirky, just like Kate.

As they pulled into the drive, people rushed from the house, shouting for Kate, embracing her as she emerged. One would think she'd spent forty days in the desert instead of two days traveling across country.

She glanced back at him more than once, her expression apologetic. "They're nuts!" she insisted.

"They love you," he said as they were swept along on a wave into the house.

"Here, dude, a beer," someone said, shoving a bottle into his hand. It wasn't even noon. But Joe

wasn't turning down a beer. He'd just taken a sip
when he heard a woman shout from the top of the
stairs. Everyone paused and looked up. *"Kaaaaate!"*
the woman cried as she flew down the stairs.

The bride, Joe realized, had appeared.

She grabbed Kate, hopping up and down, babbling about backup maids of honor. "The *dress*,"
she said.

"In the car," Kate said quickly.

Why that should make the bride cry, Joe had
no idea, but she burst into tears, and as he stood,
dumbfounded, he watched Kate, Lisa, and little
sister Cassidy with a C race upstairs.

"Get used to it," one man said to Joe. "This is
the family you're marrying into."

"Not me," Joe said quickly.

The man squinted at him. "You're not Kiefer?
Who are you, then?"

"Joe." At the man's blank look, Joe couldn't
help but laugh. "I'm the guy who was sitting next
to Kate when the plane was diverted to Dallas."

The man looked confused. "Huh?"

Joe grinned and took a swig of beer. It was going
to be an interesting day. "Is there anything to eat?"
he asked.

"Are you serious? J. J. made his ribs. You like
ribs?"

"Love 'em," Joe said and followed the man to the back of the house where he supposed he would find J. J. and his ribs.

———◦∿◦———

When Kate pulled the peach monstrosity from the bag, Lisa sank onto Cassidy's bed with a crushed expression. "It's *ruined*."

"No, no, not ruined," Kate said quickly. "Right, Cassidy? We can steam out these wrinkles, and the sash, well…maybe I just go without the sash."

"The sash makes the dress," Lisa said morosely.

"Okay. It's all okay, Lisa," Kate said, thinking frantically.

"What's *that*?" Cassidy asked, peering closely at the hem.

So did Kate. There was a yellowish, brownish stain that looked a little like mustard spreading across several inches of the hem. How had *that* happened?

"Oh my God!" Lisa cried.

"No one is going to see that!" Kate said, a little loudly. "And besides, everyone is going to be looking at you, anyway. It's *okay*!"

Lisa sniffed. She examined the wrinkled dress. One half was less poufy than the other. Lisa forced a smile. "At least *you're* here without weird stains, right? That's the important thing. Now I have all the people I love with me." She hugged Kate tightly for a moment. "And Joe is so *cute*!" she added as she let her go.

"He's gorgeous," Cassidy agreed. "Is he your boyfriend?"

"No!" Kate said instantly and then flushed. As if that wasn't bad enough, she smiled nervously. She couldn't help it.

"What's that smile?" Lisa asked, poking her.

"No smile," Kate said, still smiling. "This is not a smile."

Lisa suddenly gasped and sank down on the bed. "Ohmigod, did you guys *do* it?"

"Lisa!" Kate cried and looked at her kid sister.

"Well, did you?" Cassidy demanded. "I mean, he's so cute, and you haven't had a boyfriend in forever."

"That," she said, pointing at Cassidy, "that is *not* true."

"You sure haven't had a *good* boyfriend," Lisa agreed. "And you obviously like Joe."

"Yeah," Kate said, her smile fading. "But he's moving to Seattle."

"No way!" Cassidy exclaimed.

"That's great!" Lisa said. "You can get a job

here! It would be so great if you came back! We miss you so much!"

"I can't come back, Lisa. I have always wanted to be in publishing, and I have a great job."

"Joe and Kiefer could be friends," Lisa continued.

"They haven't even met," Kate pointed out.

"But they will!" Lisa said excitedly. "I just want you to be as happy as I am, Katie-Kate. I want you to know what I feel for Kief."

Kate snorted. "Do you know how ridiculous you sound right now? Just *yesterday* you wanted to call it off."

"You *did*?" Cassidy asked.

"Not really," Lisa said with a flick of her wrist, as if yesterday had never happened. "I never would have done it because I love Kiefer too much. And I'm going to whip him into shape."

Kate and Cassidy laughed outright.

"Seriously," Lisa said, ignoring their laughter, "I know what a great guy Kiefer is. And it's like I told you: great guys come around once in a lifetime." She looked meaningfully at Kate.

That's what Kate was afraid of.

She was relieved when her mother burst into the room and had a fit over her dress. "Well, I have my work cut out for me this afternoon, don't I?" She sighed as she examined the sash. "In the meantime, you girls are going to be late to the hairdresser! Lori is outside waiting for you."

"What about Joe?" Kate asked as Cassidy and Lisa gathered their purses.

"Don't worry about him," her mother said as she busily inspected the gown. "He's out back with your father and your Uncle Glen looking at rototillers."

Kate gasped. "Mom, *no!*"

"He'll be fine! He looked really interested," her mother insisted and began to herd them out the door. "Right now, you have bigger things to worry about. If we don't get Lisa married today, we may never have another opportunity."

"Hey!" Lisa protested, but Kate's mother had already pushed her out the door.

Chapter 10

THANKS TO THE GENEROUS NUMBER OF BATH-
rooms and irons in the Preston house, Joe was able
to clean up and shake out a suit to wear to the wedding. He hadn't seen Kate all day, but her mother
would periodically pop in to give updates. "The
girls are getting their hair done," she would say.
"The girls are at the nail salon."

Seemed to Joe they spent more time on the hair
and makeup and whatever else it was they were
doing than the wedding itself. He didn't mind,
though. He was suitably entertained by the Preston
men—father, brother, cousins, and friends. First,
there was the inspection of a broken rototiller. Next
was a rousing debate about the possibilities of the
Seattle Seahawks going All The Way next year.
Joe had been in Seattle enough to be able to toss in
a few thoughts about the NFL and the Seahawks,
and as a result, was hailed as "a guy's guy."

Joe really liked these men. They were the sort of guys he would hang out with, go to games with, get a beer with. It would be something he could look forward to, if it weren't for one small problem: Kate would be leaving soon.

The situation with Kate was difficult to think about on such a festive day. They'd shared a really weird and fabulous few days, but how could it ever be anything more than something to regale his friends with in the years to come? It wasn't as if either of them would give up a job based on one long weekend. Joe thought he understood how these things went—you meet, you hook up, you go on with life. What other choice did he have? He'd allow himself a couple of days of moping about it, but what more could he do?

He told himself to have a good time tonight. Make it count. *And then go on with your life.*

He told himself that right up to the moment he saw Kate walking down the aisle in what was perhaps the ugliest dress he'd ever seen. It was a color not found in nature. It was wrinkled, and one half was less poufy than the other. But the remarkable thing about that dress was not how ugly it was, but how fantastic Kate made it look.

In a word, *wow.* She looked gorgeous with her hair swept up and ribbons cascading down her back. In spite of the condition of the dress, it fit her beautifully, hugging every curve. To Joe, Kate looked more beautiful than the bride, more beautiful than the flowers that adorned every pew and that altar. She was…everything. Everything that came to his mind when he thought of the perfect woman.

On the arm of some sad sack as she glided down the aisle, she caught sight of Joe and her face lit with a brilliant smile. Joe felt the warmth of that smile trickle down his spine, slide into his limbs, his fingers and toes, and warm his chest like an atomic glow.

He grinned back at her, and as she moved past, she gave him a subtle wink that made him as happy as a puppy. He was admiring her slender back as she walked by and almost missed the strange yellow-brown stain at the hem of the fluffy gown. And the wrinkled sash.

His smile went even deeper.

He didn't actually hear much of the ceremony, as his entire being was focused on Kate. He couldn't take his eyes from her.

Joe rode with Mr. Preston to the reception. It was in an industrial building, but the inside had been decorated to resemble what Joe guessed was a Southern plantation, with wispy sheers of silk draped overhead, a pergola dripping in fake wisteria over the bridal table, and tall, skinny floral arrangements bursting with lilies and more silk wisteria gracing the center of each table.

"Joe, over here!" Mrs. Preston called to him from near the buffet. She had dressed in a shade of peach for the occasion. "We've put you next to Kate," she said, and leaned in next to him. "We had to move Aunt Emily, but she'll be sleeping in her soup anyway," she confided. She pointed to a seat at the bridal table.

"I don't want to displace anyone," Joe said.

"Trust me, Aunt Emily will be happier sitting with the Bergers. I don't know about them…" She smiled. "Help yourself to champagne punch. The bridal party should be here any moment."

Joe did as she suggested. He was chatting it up with another of Kate's cousins when the bridal party arrived, streaming in like peach-colored ribbons.

Joe watched as Kate stopped to greet people she knew, hugging one or two tightly, laughing with another. When she finally reached him, he handed her a glass of champagne punch.

"Wow," she said, beaming up at him. "You look so *nice,* Joe Firretti."

"And you, Kate Preston," he said, lifting his glass, "are stunning."

"Oh, stop," she said with fake modesty and

twirled around in the dress, almost knocking over a candelabra in the process. "What do you think?"

"I think," he said, looking down at the dress, "that it is the ugliest, most hideous, god-awful poufy piece of taffeta in the history of the world," he said, repeating the words she'd said to him in Dallas.

Kate burst out laughing.

"But I think it's hanging on one of the most gorgeous women I have ever seen."

Her smile was glowing. "*Thank* you," she said, curtsying. "You're just being nice." She touched her glass to his. "But I'm still going to memorize everything you just said and repeat it to myself several times a day."

"I mean it. You're beautiful," he said solemnly.

Kate's smile melted into something he understood. He was feeling the same regret and happiness, the same joy and sadness that he saw shimmering in her eyes.

Uncle Frank bumped into them at that moment and grabbed Kate up in a bear hug, giving her what Joe thought was an alarmingly rough shake in the process, yet Kate just laughed.

They were invited to be seated. Joe helped Kate into her chair and slid into his just as the happy couple arrived to rousing applause, holding each other's hands. As they dined on filet of beef, the couple was toasted with champagne for a lifetime of happiness.

Then it was Kiefer's turn to speak. "I'm not very good at this," he said, taking the mic and standing. "But as a lot of you know, I've been around awhile."

Someone in the back hooted at that, and Kiefer laughed. "Keep it down back there, Bryan. So anyway, I've been around awhile. I've had my fair share of relationships, but you know, I knew something was different when I met Lisa. I don't know if I could put a word to it, but I knew, deep down, that she was The One. To my beautiful bride," he said and leaned down to kiss her.

In the midst of a lot of oohing and aahing and cries of "Hear, hear," Joe and Kate exchanged a look. He saw the blush come up in her cheeks and felt a strange little swirl of recognition in his gut.

"My turn!" Lisa said loudly and several people chuckled. She took the mic from her husband. "As several of you know, I almost killed Kiefer this week."

The crowd laughed.

"But, honestly, I can't imagine life without him. My hope is that everyone here gets to experience the love we have for each other." She suddenly turned and looked directly at Kate and Joe. "Right, Kate?" she asked, and the crowd laughed again.

"Oh my God, she didn't just do that, did she?" Kate muttered under her breath to Joe.

"She did," he muttered back.

When the speeches were done and the toasts concluded, the band began to play. Everyone gathered around the dance floor and watched Lisa dance with her father, then with Kiefer. They swayed back and forth, sharing a private laugh.

When everyone was invited to join the dance, Joe looked at Kate and held out his hand. "Do you dance?"

"Do I dance!" she said, as if she danced for the ballet, and slipped her hand into his. "Not really."

Joe laughed. "Then that makes two of us."

He led her out onto the dance floor, took her hand and tucked it in between them, pulled her in close, and began to move.

"Hey," Kate said as they moved languidly around the dance floor. "You're a good dancer. I would not have guessed that about you."

There was so much about him that she didn't know, that he wished she knew. "What? Didn't you see me leap over the rope at the Hertz counter?"

"That was more like a hurdle," she reminded him.

"You're not so bad yourself," he said. There was an easy grace to her. "By the way," he said, "I finished your book."

She gasped with surprise; her eyes glittered happily. "When?"

"This afternoon. I had a little downtime."

"So what did you think?"

"Want to know the truth?" he asked.

Her smile faded a little. "Yes," she said. "I do." She looked as if she expected him to say something disparaging.

"I didn't want it to end," Joe said. "Don't look *that* surprised," he said, laughing at her shocked expression. "I liked those two. I wanted to know what happened after they resolved everything. What their children looked like, if she ever sorted things out with her mother."

"You *did*?"

Kate looked so happy, and Joe liked that he had made her look that way. "I did. I don't think I am going to break my lifelong habit of sticking to magazines and tech manuals, but, yes, I really enjoyed it and didn't want it to end. Do you ever feel that way?" he asked, referring to the books she edited.

Something flickered in Kate's gaze. "Yes," she said. "Actually, I'm sort of feeling that way now."

Joe sighed and pulled her in a little closer. "Me too, baby."

"You know, some might argue that this thing between us doesn't have to end, but…" Her voice trailed off. She looked a little hopeful, and that made Joe uneasy.

"But I'm here, at a new job," he said. "And you're in New York."

"And long distance never really works, does it?" she said sadly.

"Even if it did, east coast–west coast is not an easy distance to work with."

The music was ending. Kate glanced down and nodded. "I just wish… I just wish you weren't such a great guy, Joe Firretti. I wish you'd turned out to be the armrest hog from hell, you know?"

Joe couldn't help but laugh. "I kind of wish I had too," he said. He didn't like feeling as helpless and hopeless as he was right now. But he was determined not to let the evening end on a somber note. "Let's make the best of tonight."

Kate's smile returned. "What'd you have in mind?"

"Champagne to start. Then you, naked. Me, admiring you, naked." He grinned, his body stirring at just the suggestion.

"I think that could be arranged," she said coyly.

"But we have to be careful. My parents have the ears of donkeys. And you might have to jackhammer me out of this dress."

"That," he said, leaning forward, putting his mouth to her temple, "will be my great pleasure."

At half past two in the morning, Joe was lying on a cot in the library at the Preston house, his arms folded behind his head. He'd given up on Kate and figured she'd gotten cold feet in her parents' house.

But then he heard the door. He sat up, saw her slip into the library wearing a flannel pajama top that came to the top of her thighs. She closed the door very carefully behind her, then tiptoed quickly across the floor and hopped on top of him. She instantly covered his mouth with her hand. *"Shhh,"* she whispered.

Joe nodded, slipped his hand under her top, and closed his eyes as his fingers slid over smooth, warm skin. Kate began to kiss him, sinking down onto his body, her hands sliding through his hair, down his side.

Joe had the hazy thought that this was what it was supposed to be like, that the times before Kate had been nothing, just diversions, a passing of time. And when he entered her, and slid into that state of pure, pleasurable oblivion, he could think only that this was right, this was *so* right.

So right that it was screwed up.

Chapter 11

KATE WOKE TO THE SOUND OF SOMEONE rummaging around in the kitchen. She felt Joe warm on her back, his body spooned around hers. She could hear the patter of rain on the roof and wanted nothing more than to burrow deep under the covers and pretend there wasn't a world out there, or two lives on different paths.

She twisted in Joe's arms to face him, kissed his chest. Last night had been magical. Surreal, even. She hated when authors described sex as surreal, because she could never imagine how it could be so. To her, sex had always been very concrete. But last night, she'd existed outside herself, had ridden along on an enormous wave of pleasure Joe gave her. He was an excellent lover, a man of many talents, and thinking about them made her smile. She kissed his lips gently and eased off the cot.

"Hey," he said groggily, reaching for her.

"Shh," she reminded him, and touched her fingers to his lips before scurrying across the library. She opened the door, listened for the sound of anyone coming her way, and stepped out.

By the time Joe appeared—showered and dressed—Kate's extended family was present and accounted for, grazing on the leftovers from the bridal banquet.

"Honey, leave your dress," Mom was saying as Joe sauntered in, clean-shaven and impossibly handsome. "Good morning, Joe! Did you sleep well?"

He glanced at Kate. "I slept *great*," he said, and Kate almost laughed.

"There's coffee," Kate's mother said, pointing to the pot. "Anyway," she continued in Kate's direction, "I'm going to have it cleaned and boxed."

"Why, Mom?" Kate asked. "I'm never wearing it again."

"Never say 'never.' There may come some event where you need a fancy evening gown."

"You could get married in it," Cassidy offered, wiggling her eyebrows at Kate.

"Mom," Kate said wearily.

"Cassidy, leave your sister alone. She is very sensitive about peach dresses."

Kate rolled her eyes at her little sister.

"Hey, did you hear the news this morning?"

Colton asked. "They say the strike will be settled today, the blizzard is about done, and air traffic should be almost normal by Tuesday. Airports are finally opening back up."

"I guess that means no trains or cars to New York this time, Katie-Kate," her father said with a chuckle. "So, Joe, when do you start work?"

"Ah…tomorrow," he said.

"Joe, have some beef filet," Kate's mother said, steering him in the direction of the buffet where the food had been laid out. "Never accuse the Prestons of being predictable in their breakfast choices."

"Thank you," Joe said uncertainly and peered into the big aluminum pan.

"He doesn't have to eat that," Kate tried, but her mother was already waving her away.

"He doesn't mind, do you, Joe? Live on the edge, I say."

"So life goes back to normal for you two, I guess," Kate's father said from behind the morning paper.

"Oh, but Joe will come for dinner now and then, won't you, Joe?" Kate's mother chimed in.

Joe smiled, but Kate could see he wasn't feeling it. She wasn't either. What would be the point? "I'll sure try," he said, and thank God, that seemed to satisfy Kate's mom.

"It's such a shitty day," Cassidy complained.

"Language!" Kate's mother said sternly.

"Hey, Joe, do you play cards?" Colton asked. "We like to play Spades on days like this."

Kate expected him to say no, that he had to go, but Joe surprised her. With a plate laden with filet of beef and twice-baked potato, he said, "Sure!"

They spent the day with Kate's family playing cards, then working on an enormous puzzle her father had started in the dining room, and occasionally glanced at the big picture window and the rain rivulets racing down the glass.

The air felt heavy. Kate had felt a weight pressing on her all day. She knew what it was—it was the sense of an impending loss.

Late in the afternoon, as her family buzzed around the kitchen and the living area, Joe looked at Kate with sorrow in his eyes, and she knew the moment of loss had come. "I should go," he said.

Her heart sank. This was it, then, the end to the most wildly adventurous, sexy, fabulous few days she'd ever spent. "I don't want to say good-bye," she muttered helplessly.

"Then don't say it," he said, and intertwined his fingers with hers. "It's not good-bye, Kate. We'll talk, right?"

She nodded.

"What's going on?" Cassidy asked, her insanely accurate radar honing in on Joe and Kate. "Are you taking off, Joe?"

"Yeah," he said, coming to his feet. "I have an early day tomorrow." He walked away from Kate to say his good-byes to her family.

There was a lot of promising to get together, to include Joe in family gatherings in the weeks to come. But Kate didn't believe it. Her family meant well, as did Joe. But people were busy, and she could picture her family gathered here on a Sunday afternoon, and someone would mention Joe, and someone else would say, "Oh yeah, I meant to give him a call," and that would be followed by, "Let's Skype with Kate later."

And as the days and weeks went on, they would forget about him entirely. But Kate would never forget him. Never.

The rain had let up when she walked him outside. A cab was waiting at the bottom of the drive. Kate stood with her hands on her back, Joe with his hands shoved into the pockets of his jeans.

She looked at the cab, then at him. "Do you believe in fate, yet?"

He smiled wryly.

"Me either," she said. "Because if this is fate, fate sucks."

"I couldn't agree more." He shifted forward, putting his arms around her.

"Will you call me when you're in New York?" she asked in almost a whisper.

"Yes. And you'll call me when you're in Seattle, right?"

"Yes."

Joe leaned back and cupped her face. He peered into her eyes, and it felt to Kate as if he was trying to commit her to memory somehow. She reached up and wrapped her fingers around his wrist. "How can I miss you so much already when I hardly know you?"

He sighed, lowered his head, and kissed her. It was a tender, emotional kiss, and when he lifted his head, Kate dabbed at the lone tear that fell from the corner of one eye.

"I'll talk to you soon. Tomorrow, maybe." He dropped his arms from her. "Kate…I've never met anyone like you before. Thanks for…this," he said, gesturing to the two of them. "Seems so inadequate to say, but I mean it."

She knew exactly what he meant. She'd known him for all of four days now, and yet she felt like she was losing her very best friend. She shoved her hands into the back pockets of her pants to keep from grabbing on to him and holding him here. She willed herself not to get girly and teary. "Good-bye, Joe Firretti."

"Good-bye, Kate Preston."

She watched him walk down to the end of the drive. He opened the cab door and paused. He looked back at her before he got in.

Kate lifted her hand and waved.

She didn't know if he waved back because she couldn't see much through the tears that had filled her eyes.

Chapter 12

KATE HAD BEEN BACK IN NEW YORK FOR TWO weeks, and still the feeling of heaviness had not lifted from her. She'd thought that after she'd regaled the editorial staff with her wild tale of her trip to Seattle, she would fall into work and everything would fade into a warm, soft memory.

Maybe it would have, had Kate and Joe not spoken regularly.

She knew the head guy at his new company seemed impressed by Joe, and that he had a corner office. She knew he liked running in Discovery Park and he didn't like that it rained so much. He knew she had finished editing the novel he'd read and had just closed a deal for another one. They were talking, but Kate could feel a distance developing there, the inevitable flow of life carrying them away from each other. The further they drifted, the heavier the weight felt to her.

And yet, she couldn't seem to shake him. She walked to work and envisioned the dangerously handsome man who had appeared at Lisa's wedding in a dark suit, clean-shaven, and with that cute little pocket square. She walked home from work and looked at each man who passed her, trying to find one who would appeal to her the way Joe had. None of them did.

Kate still didn't know if she believed in fate, but if she did, she would want to know what exactly it was trying to do to her. Right now, she hated fate. She wanted to kick fate's ass.

One morning, seated in her cubbyhole between stacks of manuscripts and books, Kate was making herself especially crazy. Lisa was back from her two-week honeymoon and had bombarded Facebook with pictures of a tropical paradise. There was Kiefer looking toned and buff, Lisa tanned and slim.

They looked so damn happy, and that made Kate even sadder. Before she'd gotten on that plane, she wouldn't have said that marriage or commitment was at the top of her list. It hovered there somewhere, she supposed, but she'd been too focused on the move to New York, on her job, on settling in. Now, that idea was front and center. Now, she knew the void that existed in her life. It had taken the trip to show her just how much she did want love and marriage and more.

After work that day, Kate was coaxed into happy hour with a couple of people, and then to a sushi bar. She recognized the name of it—Joe had told her about it.

She returned home to her tiny walk-up apartment and looked around. Why did she think this would be so great? It looked small and dingy and… and empty. So damn empty.

The next morning, Kate more or less dragged herself to work and spent a day in meetings. By the time she was ready to go home, it had started to rain. Perfect, she thought morosely. Rain was perfect for her black mood.

She found her battered umbrella at the bottom of her bag, said good night to the security guard, and walked outside. She stood under the awning for a long moment, debating. Which would be crazier? A very crowded subway? Or trying to hail a cab?

She decided the subway was her only hope and started down the street, almost colliding with a man just standing there. Why was he standing there in the rain? Kate shot him a look—and then came to an abrupt halt.

Joe.

She was so surprised that her umbrella dropped. He caught it with his hand and propped it back up over her head. She couldn't speak; her heart was in her throat. He looked as amazing as he did in her mind's eye, every inch of him, every bit of blue in his eyes.

"Hey," he said, looking her up and down. "Don't I know you from somewhere?"

Kate stepped closer, her heart beating wildly. "Weren't you the guy sitting next to me on the plane, totally hogging the armrest?"

"Right, right," he said, smiling down at her, his eyes dancing with delight. "I remember you now. You were clogging the aisles with a big pink raft."

"What are you doing here?" she asked.

"I came to ask if you believe in fate."

Kate's breath caught.

"Because I do," he said.

"You do?"

"Yeah, I do. I believe fate put me on that plane, and I think fate led me to the best few days of my life. I think fate knocked me over the head and showed me that maybe the greatest opportunity of my life was standing right in front of me in a hideous bridesmaid dress. And I couldn't ignore her, because fate is one persistent bitch."

"Yes, yes, I know," Kate said, nodding furiously. "She's really awful." Her heart was filling up with wild, crazy hope, filling up so fast that she could hardly breathe. "So you leaped across the country to tell me that?"

Joe shook his head. He slipped his arm around her waist and drew her in to him. "I leaped to be with you, Kate."

Her heart was beating so wildly she feared she would sink to her knees. This was crazy, insane! "Wait…what about your job?"

"You know, it was an amazing opportunity," he said. "But it's not so amazing without someone to share it with. So I called my old boss and asked him for my job back."

Kate gasped.

"That call turned out pretty well. He was so thrilled to have me back that he gave me more money. Turns out, my position is pretty hard to fill."

"But what about your new job?"

Joe winced. "They weren't quite as thrilled. I think it's safe to say they were pissed. Words like 'lawsuit' and 'breach' were tossed around."

"Joe!"

"Not to worry," he said. "I hadn't signed the contract yet."

"You're moving back to New York?" she asked, afraid to believe it.

"Baby, I'm already back," he said with a wink. "And I could use a place to stay for a couple of nights."

It was a dream come true, a private hope brought to life. Kate dropped her umbrella and threw her arms around his neck and kissed him. She kissed him hard, with all the weight she'd been feeling these last few weeks. She was oblivious to the rain, oblivious to the people sailing past them. If this were a movie, little stars would burst over her head and blue birds would flit about them.

Joe was laughing when she lifted her head. "I guess that's a yes," he said.

"I love you, Joe. I know I'm not supposed to say that because I just met you, but I do, Joe, I *do*. I *love* you."

"God, Kate, I love you too," he said, burying his face in her neck. "I should have told you two weeks ago. I should never have gotten in that cab. Come on, let's get out of the rain."

He stooped down to pick up her umbrella. He put his arm around her waist and pulled her into his side. "What about ESP? Do you believe in that?" he asked.

Kate laughed. "It depends."

She believed in love. That much, she knew, and here it was, delivered by fate to her, all six feet, two inches of it.

Chapter 13

ONE YEAR LATER, ON A WET SPRING WEEKEND, Joe and Kate were married in Seattle. Lisa stood up with Kate, wearing a lovely off-the-shoulder lavender gown, which Lisa proclaimed too plain and too predictable. The reception was held at a new venue: an industrial building that had been transformed inside to look like an art museum. Or maybe it was an art museum. Joe had lost track of the details.

He was happy. Happier than he thought he could be. He was frankly amazed at how damn happy he was.

Kate was happy too. She was still amused and awed that things had happened as they had, that she'd met the man of her dreams on a flight diverted to Dallas. She was awed that she and Joe had both known, in just a few days, just *knew*, that they belonged together. What would explain that other than fate? Kate hoped that fate also had a big family in mind for them, now that she knew Joe wasn't particularly put off by people wandering in and out of the house without knocking and raiding the fridge, as her family tended to do.

They stayed at the Edgewater the night of the wedding, and their lovemaking was spectacular. The next morning they made their way to Kate's house, where the Firrettis and the Prestons had come together to dine on leftover wedding food for breakfast before the newlyweds headed off to Paris for their honeymoon. While they were dining, the clouds rolled in, swallowing up the sun.

Later still, when Colton drove them to the airport, the clouds were hanging even heavier. Kate and Joe joked about late spring blizzards and air traffic controller strikes.

The newly minted Mr. and Mrs. Firretti checked their bags. "Are you sure you want to carry that on?" Joe asked, looking at the enormous tote bag Kate was holding. "Yes," she said. "It's got everything we need. Books, iPad, toothbrushes, change of underwear—"

"Okay, okay," he said. "Just please don't tell me it has a tuna-fish sandwich in it."

"No!" Kate said. "I'll buy that at a kiosk or something." She smiled at his look of horror.

They made it through security and wandered up to their gate. They glanced up at the board. *Delayed*, it said.

"Wait here," Joe said and walked up to the counter and spoke to the airline agent. He returned a moment later, a funny little smile on his face.

"So what's the delay?" Kate asked.

"Indefinite. Seems there is an unexpected weather event in Europe and the plane coming in is being diverted."

Kate blinked. And Mr. and Mrs. Firretti burst into laughter.

Read on for an excerpt from the contemporary romance debut from *New York Times* bestselling author Grace Burrowes:

A Single Kiss

"SHE HAD THAT TWITCHY, NOTHING-GETS-BY-HER quality." MacKenzie Knightley flipped a fountain pen through his fingers in a slow, thoughtful rhythm. "I liked her."

Trenton Knightley left off doodling Celtic knots on his legal pad to peer at his older brother. "You liked her? You *liked* this woman? You don't like anybody, particularly females."

"I respected her," Mac said, "which, because you were once upon a time a husband, you ought to know is more important to the ladies than whether I like them."

"Has judge written all over him," James, their younger brother, muttered. "The criminals in this town would howl to lose their best defense counsel, though. I liked the lady's résumé, and I respected it too."

Gail Russo, the law firm's head of human resources, thwacked a file onto the conference table.

"Don't start, gentlemen. Mac has a great idea. Hannah Stark interviewed very well, better than any other candidate we've considered in the past six months. She's temped with all the big boys in Baltimore, has sterling academic credentials, and—are you listening?—is available."

"The best kind," James murmured.

Trent used Gail's folder to smack James on the shoulder, though James talked a better game of tomcat than he strutted.

"You weren't even here to interview her, James, and she's under consideration for your department."

"The press of business…" James waved a languid hand. "My time isn't always my own."

"You were pressing business all afternoon?" Mac asked from beyond retaliatory smacking range.

"The client needed attention," James replied. "Alas for poor, hardworking me, she likes a hands-on approach. Was this Hannah Stark young, pretty, and single, and can she bill sixty hours a week?"

"We have a decision to make," Gail said. "Do we dragoon Hannah Stark into six months in domestic relations then let her have the corporate law slot, or do we hire her for corporate when the need is greater in family law? Or do we start all

over and this time advertise for a domestic relations associate?"

Domestic law was Trent's bailiwick, but because certain Child In Need of Assistance attorneys could not keep their closing arguments to
less than twenty minutes per case, Trent hadn't
interviewed the Stark woman either.

"Mac, you really liked her?" Trent asked.

"She won't tolerate loose ends," Mac said.
"She'll work her ass off before she goes to court.
The judges and opposing counsel will respect that,
and anybody who can't get along with you for
their boss for six months doesn't deserve to be in
the profession."

"I agree with Mac." James dropped his chair
forward, so the front legs hit the carpet. "I'm
shorthanded, true, but not that shorthanded. Let's
ask her to pitch in for six months in domestic, then
let her have the first shot at corporate if we're still
swamped in the spring."

"Do it, Trent," Mac said, rising. "Nobody had
a bad thing to say about her, and you'll be a better mentor for her first six months in practice than
Lance Romance would be. And speaking of domestic relations, shouldn't you be getting home?"

～～～

Grace Stark bounded into the house ahead of her mother, while Hannah brought up the rear with two grocery bags and a shoulder-bag-cum-purse. Whenever possible, for the sake of the domestic tranquility and the budget, Hannah did her shopping without her daughter's company.

Hannah's little log house sat on the shoulder of a rolling western Maryland valley, snug between the cultivated fields and the wooded mountains. She took a minute to stand beside the car and appreciate the sight of her own house—hers and the bank's—and to draw in a fortifying breath of chipper air scented with wood smoke.

The Appalachians rose up around the house like benevolent geological dowagers, surrounding Hannah's home with maternal protectiveness. Farther out across the valley, subdivisions encroached on the family farms, but up here much of the land wouldn't perc, and the roads were little more than widened logging trails.

The property was quiet, unless the farm dogs across the lane took exception to the roosters, and the roosters on the next farm over took exception to the barking dogs, and so on.

Still, it was a good spot to raise a daughter who enjoyed a busy imagination and an appreciation for nature. Damson Valley had a reputation as a

peaceful, friendly community, a good place to
set down roots. Hannah's little house wasn't that
far from the Y, the park, and the craft shops that
called to her restricted budget like so many sirens.

The shoulder bag dropped down to Hannah's
elbow as she wrestled the door open while jug-
gling grocery bags.

"Hey, Mom. Would you make cheese shells
again? I promise I'll eat most of mine."

"Most?" Hannah asked as she put the milk in the
fridge. The amount she'd spent was appalling, considering how tight money was. Thank heavens Grace
thought pasta and cheese sauce was a delicacy.

"A few might fall on the floor," Grace said,
petting a sleek tuxedo cat taking its bath in the
old-fashioned dry sink.

"How would they get on the floor?"

"They might fall off my plate." Grace cuddled
the cat, who bore up begrudgingly for about three
seconds, then vaulted to the floor. Grace took a
piece of purple yarn from a drawer, trailing an end
around the cat's ears.

"Cats have to eat too, you know," Grace said.
"They love cheese. It says so on TV, and Henry
says his mom lets him feed cheese to Ginger."

"Ginger is a dog. She'd eat kittens if she got
hungry enough." The groceries put away, Hannah

set out place mats and cutlery for two on the kitchen table. "You wouldn't eat kittens just because Henry let Ginger eat kittens, would you?"

Did all parents make that same dumb argument?

And did all parents put just a few cheesy pieces of pasta in the cat dish? Did all parents try to assuage guilt by buying *fancy 100 percent beef wieners* instead of hot dogs?

"Time to wash your hands, Grace," Hannah said twenty minutes later. "Hot dogs are ready, so is your cat food."

"But, Mom," Grace said, looping the string around the drawer pull on the dry sink, "all I did was pet Geeves, and she's just taken a whole bath. Why do I always have to wash my hands?"

"Because Geeves used the same tongue to wash her butt as she did to wash her paws, and because I'm telling you to."

Grace tried to frown mightily at her mother but burst out giggling. "You said butt, and you're supposed to ask."

"Butt, butt, butt," Hannah chorused. "Grace, would you please wash your hands before Geeves and I gobble up all your cheesy shells?"

They sat down to their mac and cheese, hot dogs, and salad, a time Hannah treasured—she treasured any time with her daughter—and dreaded. Grace could be stubborn when tired or when her day had gone badly.

"Grace, please don't wipe your hands on your shirt. Ketchup stains, and you like that shirt."

"When you were a kid, did you wipe your hands on your shirt?" Grace asked while chewing a bite of hot dog.

"Of course, and I got reminded not to, unless I was wearing a ketchup-colored shirt, in which case I could sneak a small smear."

Grace started to laugh with her mouth full, and Hannah was trying to concoct a *request* that would encourage the child to desist, when her cell phone rang. This far into the country, the expense of a landline was necessary because cell reception was spotty, though tonight the signal was apparently strong enough.

"Hello, Stark's."

"Hi, this is Gail Russo from Hartman and Whitney. Is this Hannah?"

The three bites of cheesy shells Hannah had snitched while preparing dinner went on a tumbling run in her tummy. "This is Hannah."

"I hope I'm not interrupting your dinner, Hannah, but most people like to hear something as soon as possible after an interview. I have good news, I think."

"I'm listening."

Grace used her fork to draw a cat in her ketchup.

"You interviewed with two department heads and a partner," Gail said, "which is our in-house rule before a new hire, and they all liked you."

Hannah had liked the two department heads. The partner, Mr. MacKenzie Knightley, had been charm-free, to put it charitably. Still, he'd been civil, and when he'd asked if she had any questions, Hannah had the sense he'd answer with absolute honesty.

The guy had been good-looking, in a six-foot-four, dark-haired, blue-eyed way that did not matter in the least.

"I'm glad they were favorably impressed," Hannah said as Grace finished her mac and cheese.

"Unfortunately for you, we also had a little excitement in the office today. The chief associate in our domestic relations department came down with persistent light-headedness. She went to her obstetrician just to make sure all was well with her pregnancy and was summarily sent home and put on complete bed rest."

"I'm sorry to hear that." *Not domestic relations*. If there were a merciful God, Hannah would never again set foot in the same courtroom with a family law case. Never.

"She's seven months along, so we're looking at another two months without her, then she'll be out on maternity leave. It changed the complexion of the offer we'd like to make you."

"An offer is good." An offer would become an absolute necessity in about one-and-a-half house payments.

Grace was disappearing her hot dog with as much dispatch as she'd scarfed up her mac and cheese.

"We'd like you to start as soon as possible, but put you in the domestic relations department until Janelle can come back in the spring. We'll hire somebody for domestic in addition to her, but you're qualified, and the need, as they say, is now."

"Domestic relations?" Prisoners sentenced to life-plus-thirty probably used that same tone of voice.

"Family law. Our domestic partner is another Knightley brother, but he's willing to take any help he can get. He was in court today when Janelle packed up and went home, otherwise you might have interviewed with him."

"I see."

What Hannah saw was Grace, helping herself to her mother's unfinished pasta.

"You'd be in domestic for only a few months, Hannah, and Trent Knightley is the nicest guy you'd ever want to work for. He takes care of his people, and you might find you don't want to leave domestic in the spring, though James Knightley is also a great boss."

Gail went on to list benefits that included a signing bonus. Not a big one, but by Hannah's standards, it would clear off all the bills, allow for a few extravagances, and maybe even the start of a savings account.

God in heaven, a savings account.

"Mom, can I have another hot dog?" Grace stage-whispered her request, clearly trying to be good.

Except there wasn't another hot dog. Hannah had toted up her grocery bill as she'd filled her cart, and there wasn't another damned hot dog.

Thank God my child is safe for another day... But how safe was Grace in a household where even hot dogs were carefully rationed?

Hannah covered the phone. "You may have mine, Grace."

"Thanks!"

"Hannah? Are you there?"

A beat of silence, while Hannah weighed her daughter's need for a second hot dog against six months of practicing law in a specialty Hannah loathed, dreaded, and despised.

"I accept the job, Gail, though be warned I will transfer to corporate law as soon as I can."

"You haven't met Trent. You're going to love him."

No, Hannah would not.

Gail went on to explain details—starting day, parking sticker, county bar identification badge—and all the while, Hannah watched her hot dog disappear and knew she was making a terrible mistake.

———

"Trent Knightley is a fine man, and his people love him," Gail said, passing Hannah's signing bonus check across the desk. "The only folks who don't like to see him coming are opposing counsel, and even they respect him."

"He sounds like an ideal first boss."

What kind of fine man wanted to spend his days breaking up families and needed the head of HR singing his praises at every turn?

The entire first morning was spent with Gail, filling out forms—and leaving some spaces on those forms blank. Gail took Hannah to lunch, calling it de rigueur for a new hire.

"In fact," Gail said between bites of a chicken Caesar, "you will likely be taken out to lunch by each of the three partners, though Mac tends to be less social than his brothers. You ordering dessert?"

People who could afford gym memberships ordered dessert.

"I'd like to get back to work if you don't mind, Gail. I have yet to meet the elusive Trent Knightley, and if he should appear in the office this afternoon, I don't want to be accused of stretching lunch on my first day."

Not on any day. If Hannah had learned anything temping for the Baltimore firms, it was that law firms were OCD about time sheets and billable hours.

"Hannah, you are not bagging groceries. No one, and I mean no one, will watch your time as long as your work is getting done, your time sheet is accurate, and most of your clients aren't complaining. Get over the convenience-store galley slave mentality."

Gail paid the bill with a corporate card, and no doubt the cost of lunch would have bought many packages of fancy 100 percent beef wieners.

"Don't sweat the occasional long lunch," Gail said as they drove back to the office. "Trent takes as many as anyone else, and the way he eats, he'd better."

Gail's comment had Hannah picturing Mr. Wonderful Boss, Esq., as a pudgy middle-aged fellow who put nervous clients at ease and probably used a cart and a caddy when he played golf with the judges.

———~~~———

Hannah finished arranging the fresh flowers that had just been delivered to her office, her sole extravagance as the proud recipient of a signing bonus. The florist had recommended the purple glads, and for good reason, for they were splendid specimens. Hannah pulled out one long, magenta-lavender blossom to share with Grace.

Gino, the beefy Italian facility manager, had delivered a banker's box piled high with every imaginable office supply and promised Hannah he'd have her computer installed by tomorrow morning. Her office was a tidy, impersonal space but for the flower arrangement, and she liked it that way—even when temping, a lawyer learned that clients got nosy. She wrapped the gladiolus in a wet paper towel, then spotted a volume of *Maryland Family Law* on her credenza.

A poo-poo brown book for a poo-poo brown subject, Grace would say.

Still, it was a reference book that belonged in the boss's shelves. Hannah had taken a moment to assess Trenton Knightley's private office, and found it cozy, like a den or study, more baronial than palatial. The Oriental rug and upholstered furniture went with her well-fed, middle-aged, avuncular image of him. Then too, if he kept the firm's family law library in printed book form, maybe he was a bit of a cyberphobe.

Some of the older attorneys were.

Hannah approached the door to the boss's office, book in one hand, flower in the other. A man's voice coming from within stopped her before she would have barged through the slightly open door.

"So what are you doing tonight?" the guy asked, voice pitched intimately, the inflection lazy and personal. A beautiful, sexy voice completely inappropriate for a law office during business hours.

"Do you think he could stand to part with you for an hour?" the man asked.

Hannah told herself to put the damned book back another time, but curiosity held her in place.

"I'm in the mood for a ride." *A ride? How crude was that?* "I was stuck all day on a nasty case, and I need to change gears. The best way I know to do that is spend some time with my favorite girl."

Oh, for cryin' in a bucket. Hannah turned to go, but some flicker of light or shadow must have given her away. The door swung open.

"I'll be there in less than an hour," he said into a cell phone. "Go ahead and eat something—you'll need your energy." He slipped the phone into his pocket and smiled at Hannah. His jacket was off, his shirt sleeves cuffed back, and his tie—a stylized image of a white horse galloping out of a crashing blue surf—was loosened.

The informality of the guy's attire only emphasized that fact that he was drop-dead-of-an-estrogen-coronary gorgeous. Tall, dark, and handsome, three for three. His sable hair was a tad long, his facial architecture a touch dramatic. Even white teeth arranged in a shark-smile, and blue, blue eyes finished off a walking assault to a woman's composure.

Hannah stood in the doorway, *Family Law* in one hand, a perfectly phallic flower in the other.

Her mouth snapped shut.

"Hello," he said, still exuding the air of happy anticipation he'd had on the phone. "Is that flower for me?"

"You got some nerve, buddy." Hannah plowed past him. "If you must arrange your assignations on company time, then at least do it someplace

other than the boss's office, and no, this flower is
not for you."

Those bachelor-button blue eyes began to
dance. "Perhaps we'd best introduce ourselves before we're handing out citations for unprofessional
conduct. Trent Knightley, director, Domestic
Relations. And you would be?"

Unemployed. *Again.*

"Toast," Hannah muttered, setting the book on
the pale oak coffee table and seeing her new, im-
proved grocery budget evaporate before her eyes.
"I would be utter toast."

"You're my new hire," he said, the smile dip-
ping into a frown. "Heather? Helen? No…"

Was it a good thing that he couldn't recall the
name of the associate he probably intended to
work to death?

She dutifully extended a hand. "Hannah Stark."

"Hannah," he said, taking her hand in his and
not shaking it, but holding it as he studied her.
"Have a seat. I am remiss for not greeting you in
person, but depositions wait for no man or lady.
How was your first day?"

Lawyers could be remiss; other people dropped
the ball or screwed up.

The mischief in his gaze was gone, which was
a relief. Everybody had said he was nice; nobody

had said he was a gorgeous, womanizing, flirting—

She took a seat while he folded his length into a wing chair, stretched out long legs, and crossed them at the ankle.

"My *assignation* isn't for an hour," he reminded her. "Spare me five minutes and tell me about your day."

Cross-examination, of course.

"Busy," Hannah said, "but unremarkable. My forms are executed for HR, my office is outfitted, I did lunch with Gail. I spent some time this afternoon trying to track down a case for another associate—I forget the gentleman's name."

"Viking blond? Toothpaste-commercial smile?"

"He has the child support docket." Hannah had seen no toothpaste-commercial smiles outside present company. "Matthew?"

"Gerald Matthews."

"Right. Gerald. His client can prove he had a vasectomy prior to the child's birth—the client, not Gerald—and the procedure hasn't reversed itself since. Gerald thinks there's some relevant case law."

"If the case is coming up Friday and Gerald hasn't started his research, then perhaps you'd like to handle it?"

A silence spread, with Hannah eyeing her

flower, while her boss eyed her. This was the price of fancy 100 percent beef wieners. She didn't want to touch the child support docket, neither did she want to admit her reluctance to Mr. Divorces-Are-Us.

"How about not quite yet?" Hannah hedged.

"Fair enough. Why the flower, Hannah Stark?"

Damned lawyer. He'd dropped back into that sexy, conspiring, you-can-trust-me tone he'd used on the phone.

"They're pretty."

"You sent them to yourself?"

She fingered the last blossom, feeling foolish and angry, because a good lawyer could do this. Lead the witness down one path of inquiry, then ambush them from an entirely different direction.

"I like flowers."

She liked signing bonuses, too, and making her mortgage payments on time.

"How about you plan to observe Gerald on happy pappy day?"

"I beg your pardon?"

"We hear all child support matters on Friday in Damson County. It's payday for a lot of people, so it maximizes the chance of some money coming in against arrearages. A Friday docket also gives the folks who are locked up for nonsupport the weekend to come up with the money so they don't miss as much work getting processed out."

The science of lives coming unraveled was part of the reason Hannah loathed family law. "You want me to handle child support cases?"

"Gerald has the docket well in hand, but, yes, I'll want you trained for it, because we should all be able to back each other up. You and I did not get a chance to interview each other, Hannah. My philosophy with the people working for me is to give them what they need to do a good job, then leave them alone to do it. With you, I'll have to be more hands on."

Not a hint of an innuendo of a possibility of flirtation underlay the words *hands on*.

"Because?"

"Because you have no courtroom experience, and family law is litigation intensive."

She'd been in courtrooms since she'd turned three years old. "You and the other three associates can't do the courtroom cases?"

He rose and took the flower from her, poured a glass of water from a pitcher on the windowsill, and balanced the gladiolus in its makeshift vase. The long stem leaned precariously against a thriving rhododendron, but was at least spared death-by-wilting before Hannah even got it home.

"Most new associates are chomping at the bit to get on their white chargers and be God's gift to the courtroom," he said. "I gather you're not."

The problem was not litigation—Hannah was as willing to go to court as the next attorney—the problem was family law.

"I will be honest," Hannah said, because honesty was expedient in this case, and because he'd looked after Grace's flower. "I want to pull my share of the load until I can safely slide over to corporate services. In a divorcing family, the children can't be in two different households at the same time. It's a zero-sum game that isn't a game at all."

"Gail warned me you were reluctant. Not too reluctant, I trust?"

"No, sir," Hannah said, getting to her feet.

"No, Trent."

"I beg your pardon?"

"Hannah, before you let my little brother work your fanny off this spring, you and I will be eating cold pepperoni with black olives out of the same pizza box. We'll get into yelling matches about litigation strategy. We'll drive to and from the courthouse together at least once a week. I might pick up your dry cleaning. You might share your worst professional fears with me or pass off to me the client who couldn't keep his hands to himself. Call. Me. Trent."

What to say? Yes, sir? "Yes, Trent, but I draw the line at anchovies and pineapple."

"Sit down for one more minute, and let me explain something to you." He did not make it a question. Grace would have told him so.

Hannah dropped into her seat, though the clock on the wall said if she didn't want to be late to pick up Grace—with all the misery that would cause— then she couldn't afford any protracted lectures.

"Mac handles criminal law, but he's never committed a crime. James does corporate and property, though he's never owned a business except for this one, and he owns exactly one piece of ground. I, however, practice family law and was raised in a family. So were you—good, bad, indifferent, or wonderful, every family law attorney has family, and baggage as a result."

After nearly two decades with the most over-worked therapists the taxpayer could inflict on foster children, Hannah still had to get the baggage lecture from her new boss.

"What's your point?"

"You'll get your buttons pushed in this business, Hannah Stark, by the cases, the clients, oppos-ing counsel, the judges. We aren't like the social

workers and counselors who have a built-in chain
of command to support them when they're losing
their emotional balance, but we do have common
sense. When you're in over your head, you come
to me, and we'll address it. When I have a tough
case, we staff it and get the benefit of everybody's
wisdom. The point is you will not be in the deep
end alone with the sharks. I'll be there with you, if
I'm doing my job."

Family law *was* the deep end, and she was already in it and late to pick up her kid.

"This is what Gail meant when she said you
were good to work for, isn't it?"

"She said that?"

"Said everybody loves to work for you."

"Probably because I'm off at court so much."
He smiled, the corners of his eyes crinkling. This
curving of his lips was more charming than his
"Hi, I'm your new boss" version. "I'll tell Gerald
to expect you to shadow him this week, but for
tomorrow, why not watch my deposition?"

"May I take the case file home with me tonight?" And leave in the next six minutes?

"You may not," he said, his smile broadening.
"You're already doing research for Gerald he
ought to do himself. If he's swamped, he also has
a paralegal to help him, or he could have come

to me. Pace yourself for the long haul, Hannah. Enough cases go home with you whether you want them to or not. Now get your things, and I'll walk you to your car. I'm scheduled to freeze my backside off trail riding under the full moon tonight."

That kind of ride? Well, then, maybe it was OK to like the guy, even if he was down-to-earth, good-looking, and willing to brave the full moon on a weeknight.

"No need to walk me to my car, thank you," Hannah said, getting to her feet. Her answer might have been different if he'd made it a question.

"Suit yourself," he said, rising as well. "Deposition starts at nine. We'll leave here around eight thirty, and, Hannah?"

"Sir?"

He raised an eyebrow.

"Trent?"

"Welcome aboard." He shook her hand again, then let her go.

The First Kiss

A Sweetest Kisses Novel

by Grace Burrowes

New York Times and *USA Today* Bestselling Author

The first kiss is the one that means a fresh start

Classical pianist Vera Waltham is quiet, cautious, and fiercely protective of her young daughter, but she lets down her guard enough to strike up an unlikely friendship with business law expert James Knightley. James's past comes between them when Vera learns exactly how big a tomcat he has been, but when she and her daughter are in danger, it's to James she turns…

Praise for Grace Burrowes:

"Warmth, sensuality, and humor infuse Burrowes's writing." —*Booklist*

"Grace Burrowes weaves her magic with eloquent, revealing words and subtle humor." —*Long and Short Reviews*

For more Grace Burrowes, visit:

www.sourcebooks.com

Kiss Me Hello

A Sweetest Kisses Novel

by Grace Burrowes

New York Times and *USA Today* Bestselling Author

—◆—

Sidonie Lindstrom's hands and heart are full—she's been uprooted from the urban life she loves, she's grieving for her brother while raising her foster son Luis, and she's trying to find a job with meaning.

But her burdens feel lighter when she meets MacKenzie Peckham. Their attraction is powerful and unexpected. Life is perfect...until Sid learns that Mac hasn't been completely honest about his job. When problems arise with Luis's foster care situation, she must decide: Can she trust Mac again, when she has so much more to lose?

—◆—

Praise for Grace Burrowes:

"Burrowes's great writing and ability to bring her characters to life with subtle power and authenticity enhance an emotionally charged romance." —*Kirkus*

"I love her style of writing and the stories she tells have depth and emotion that will capture your heart and mind." —*Night Owl Reviews*

For more Grace Burrowes, visit:

www.sourcebooks.com

The Deepest Night

by Kara Braden

———

When everything you love is on the line...

The Isles of Scilly off the coast of England are remote, windswept, and wild. They're the perfect place for Ray Powell to recuperate after the toughest Afghanistan mission the military contractor has ever run. Except instead of the peace and quiet he so desperately needs, he's faced with a beautiful American woman who instantly challenges his iron control.

It's best to proceed with caution...

Seeking her own safe haven, Michelle Cole is intrigued and flustered by the intensely compelling and irresistible man.

As their cautious friendship slowly builds into simmering attraction, their hearts and souls are about to be broken open—if they'll allow it.

———

"This smashing sequel shows that respectful communication is downright scorching... This sweet contemporary will appeal to romance fans who like their heroes powerful and smitten and their heroines capable and genuine." —*Publishers Weekly* Starred Review

"The characters and plot are well developed, and *The Deepest Night* can stand alone." —*Booklist*

For more Kara Braden, visit:

www.sourcebooks.com

Return to You

A Montgomery Brothers Novel

by Samantha Chase

New York Times and *USA Today* Bestselling Author

She will never forget their past...

He can't stop thinking about their future...

James Montgomery has achieved everything he'd hoped for in life...except marrying the girl of his dreams. After a terrible accident, Selena Ainsley left ten years ago. She took his heart with her, and she's never coming back. But it's becoming harder and harder for him to forget their precious time together, and James can't help but wonder what he would do if they could ever meet again.

What readers are saying about Samantha Chase:

"Samantha Chase really knows how to tell a story."

"Perfect romance! Love it, love it, love it!"

For more Samantha Chase, visit:

www.sourcebooks.com

About the Author

Julia London is the *New York Times* and *USA Today* bestselling author of more than two dozen novels, including the Cedar Springs contemporary series, the Secrets of Hadley Green historical romance series, and numerous other works. She is a four-time finalist for the prestigious RITA Award for excellence in romantic fiction, and RT Book Club Award recipient for Best Historical Romance. She lives in Austin, Texas.